Well written and insanely hot... One of the things I liked best about this book was the way Cartwright had of explaining the BDSM lifestyle... I'm definitely looking forward to the next installment in this Mastered series and will be rereading With This Collar while I wait, for it is a great scorching love story well worth reading at any time. ~ *Whipped Cream*

This very spicy read gives a beautiful exposition of one woman's journey into an erotic world that she knew very little of... There are very hot scenes that demonstrate some of the techniques that can be applied but this is also a delicious love story and I look forward to reading more titles from this gifted author. ~ *Night Owl Romance*

Ms. Cartwright managed to deliver yet another amazing BDSM story. I enjoyed reading WITH THIS COLLAR immensely. It is well written and perfectly paced. The characters are great—even the side ones that I can't wait to read more about—and there are just enough witty lines to highlight the sassy part of their personalities...I give 4.5 stars for the first book of the Mastered series. Can't wait to read more.
~ *The Romance Reviews*

With This Collar by Sierra Cartwright is a beautifully written BDSM story that contains the heart and soul of the BDSM world. Ms. Cartwright did not miss a beat in creating Master Marcus and Julia... As far as the plot goes, this is a rock solid read that will heat you up in a Nano second! The characters demand your attention as the story unfolds. I enjoyed the fact that Julia fights back. What can I say…I like a woman with gumption. *LOL!* Ms. Cartwright is a master in her own right when it comes to writing the BDSM genre. She gets an A++ from me. With This Collar is a must have for anyone's BDSM collection. Bring on the next book in the series! ~ *BlackRaven's Reviews*

Total-E-Bound Publishing books by Sierra Cartwright:

Mastered
With This Collar

Signed, Sealed & Delivered
Bound and Determined
Her Two Doms

Anthologies
Naughty Nibbles: This Time
Naughty Nibbles: Fed Up
Bound Brits: S&M 101
Subspace: Three-way Tie
Night of the Senses: Voyeur
Bound to the Billionaire: Bared to Him

Seasonal Collections
Halloween Hearthrobs: Walk on the Wild Side
Homecoming: Unbound Surrender

Clasndestine Classics
Jane Eyre

Mastered

ON HIS TERMS

SIERRA CARTWRIGHT

On His Terms
ISBN # 978-1-78184-599-8
©Copyright Sierra Cartwright 2013
Cover Art by Posh Gosh ©Copyright 2013
Interior text design by Claire Siemaszkiewicz
Total-E-Bound Publishing

Published in 2013 by Total-E-Bound Publishing, Think Tank, Ruston Way, Lincoln, LN6 7FL, United Kingdom.

Total-E-Bound Publishing is an imprint of Total-E-Ntwined Limited.

ON HIS TERMS

Chapter One

"There he is."

"Where?" Chelsea Barton craned her head to get a look at Master Alexander Monahan.

"Near the fireplace," her friend Sara said.

Chelsea glanced in that direction. Dressed in blue jeans, a long-sleeved, western-style shirt, a black leather vest, a silver bolo tie and a cowboy hat, he didn't fit her image of a BDSM trainer. His height, though, over six feet tall, was definitely what she'd expected.

"Quit staring!" Sara said in a harsh whisper. "A good sub doesn't behave that way."

That didn't stop Chelsea. Rules were helpful for other people. As for her, she knew what she wanted and she ruthlessly pursued it. And she wanted Master Alexander to make her into the perfect sub—or at least passable enough that no one noticed if she wasn't really all that into it. That was step one in Project Snag Evan C.

Master Evan C was a rocker whose band was climbing the charts. With the right PR firm—hers, if she could sign him—he could become a household name. As a double bonus, her firm would gain some real credibility by signing Evan C. But first she needed to snare his attention. And so far, her efforts had been a dismal failure.

She'd met him at a party six months ago, and she'd developed a certifiable fangirl crush on him. She masturbated to fantasies of him tying her up and fucking her hard. She wanted him, bad. And not just as a client, but also as a Dom. What could be more fabulous than career success and having a sexy man to boot?

Sara, always the unwelcome pragmatist, had advised Chelsea to forget her ideas. Master Evan C liked well-trained submissives, women who perfectly subjugated their needs to suit his. Which, as Sara pointed out, really wasn't Chelsea. Chelsea was headstrong and determined, a driven type A-plus personality who chewed antacid for breakfast, had rampant insomnia, and hadn't taken a vacation in over five years. That Master Evan C discarded women like the scarves he wore while performing made her all the more resolved to be the one to win him.

That was where Master Alexander came in.

According to Sara, he used to be a trainer, and he was still well respected. He didn't get emotionally involved with subs, and he was one of the best. That he was no longer in the business didn't deter her.

"He's looking this way," Sara said, unnecessarily.

"And he's alone, finally," Chelsea replied. When she'd heard that Sara and her Dom had been invited to Master Alexander's birthday party at the Den, Master Damien's luxury mountain retreat, Chelsea had begged, pleaded and cajoled for an invitation.

At first, Sara had refused. She hadn't wanted to be part of any more of Chelsea's schemes. While Chelsea didn't blame her friend — after all, their last escapade had earned Sara a punishment beating from her Dom — Chelsea was set on her course. "If you'll excuse me..."

"Remember, you promised not to use my name. You don't know me."

She looked at Sara. "Have we been introduced?"

"Bitch," Sara said.

"Love you, too, girlfriend." After setting her shoulders, Chelsea headed straight for Master Alexander.

A couple stopped to talk to him. With a sigh, she paused to grab a glass of wine from a passing server. She was woman enough to appreciate the hottie. He wore a bow tie, but no shirt. He could have been poured into that pair of dress slacks. The material revealed his muscular thighs as well as his hot rear. And she supposed it was possible he had oil rubbed on his bare chest.

He bowed and said, "Enjoy your evening, madam."

Maybe she'd hire this crew for her next event. It would certainly be a shocker, get her some much-appreciated press.

Rather than taking a drink, she rolled the glass between her palms and waited. Finally the couple moved off.

She put down the drink, pulled back her shoulders, and began to move towards him. Damn, the cowboy hat just made him look like an outlaw.

He rested his forearm on the mantelpiece as she approached. Even from several feet away, he exuded power. Chelsea was weaned on bravado, and she had to call on that to keep moving forwards when she became aware of the way he watched her. His focus was intent and purposeful, and he casually glanced from the toes of her pumps to the top of the shiny clips she'd placed in her short hair.

He didn't greet her. Instead, he waited. That didn't surprise her. She'd done plenty of research on him. He hadn't got to where he was in the financial world by rushing to judgement. "Mr Monahan, I'm Chelsea Barton." She extended her hand and gave him her most dazzling, dentist-whitened smile. The look was practised. She could charm anyone with it. "I wanted to wish you a very happy birthday."

"Thank you." Finally, he dropped his arm and accepted her hand.

His grip was warm, firm, reassuring. Electricity all but danced up her spine. This close, he was gorgeous. Small lines were etched next to his eyes, and his lips were firm and full. The crazy notion of kissing him skipped through her mind before she ruthlessly shoved it away. She had a business proposition for him, nothing more.

He released her. "Who are you here with?"

"I came with a friend," she hedged.

"Are you always evasive?"

"Are you always so direct?"

He folded his arms across his chest. "Save us both some time, Ms Barton. Let's cut through the bullshit. It's my birthday, my party and I approved the guest list. I saw you speaking with Sara. And I've met everyone else whose date I didn't know, so I assume Sara invited you. And since she didn't introduce you and is pretending not to see you talking to me, I assume you wanted to meet me for a specific reason."

"A lot of people want to meet you, I take it?"

"I don't play games. You've got thirty seconds."

Suddenly she wished she'd taken a drink of that wine. "You're right," she confessed. This wasn't going how she'd envisioned. "I wanted to meet you. But it's not what you think. I own a company named You're The Star. We do PR."

"Monahan Capital has a PR firm."

"That could have done a better job of spinning the Bartholomew deal initially, but they've done a good job of managing the conversation since then. If you did a couple of events in the community, such as a fundraiser, your positive press would shove the other headlines off the first page of the search engines. But that's not my point." Since he was still listening, she kept talking. "I looked you up because I want you to train me as a submissive." Her research had indicated he was inflexible, a formidable foe in the business arena despite his recent setbacks.

She was tall, especially in her spiked 'fuck-me' heels, but he still towered over her by a number of inches. Since she was accustomed to looking men in the eye as they spoke, looking up at him was a little disconcerting. For one of the first times in her life, she felt small, overpowered. "Word in the community is that you're the best."

"At one time that was true."

From his mouth, that didn't sound arrogant.

"But I'm quite sure you've heard I don't train anymore."

She pushed back the trepidation that had started doing the backstroke in her veins. The years had taught her a valuable lesson—when she wasn't getting what she wanted, she needed to turn up the charm. She placed her hand lightly on his arm. When he didn't react, she continued, "I'm sure a man as discerning as you has high expectations and demands excellence. I understand that a price tag is attached to that. I will write you a cheque tonight, Mr Monahan. Name your price."

He didn't respond to her tactics. In fact, his jawline could have been chiselled from granite. "I'm not for sale, Ms Barton."

She gave up on charm and dropped her hand. She noticed that Master Evan C and a woman were heading down the stairs. Although she hadn't seen it, she understood Master Damien had a dungeon with some private playrooms. She angled her chin, vowing not to fail. "You're a businessman. You, better than anyone, knows everyone has a price."

"What's yours?" he countered. "Would you sell your soul for success?"

"That's harsh. You don't know anything about me."

"I know you will use manipulation in order to get what you want. Machiavelli was your inspiration, perhaps?"

She pulled back.

"If you want this conversation to continue, be honest." His tone was as icy as an Arctic cold front.

Chelsea had not expected this to be so difficult. She'd figured most Doms would love to have a sub begging for their attention. The money she'd offered should have sealed the deal. "I want Evan C to hire my company and accept me as his submissive."

"And you think some training will get his attention?"

"It will."

"You sound convinced."

She recalled the party they'd been at. "He snubbed me once because I was too new." Seeing him toss his scarf over his shoulder as he'd walked away had stung.

"What kind of experience do you have?" Master Alexander asked.

"Not much," she admitted reluctantly.

"Be specific."

"How much information do you want?"

He captured her chin, ignoring the way she'd tipped it stubbornly. His fingers were strong and firm, as unrelenting as the glint in his brown eyes. "I'll tell you when I've heard enough."

She tried, and failed, to hide her shiver. For the first time in her life, she wondered if she hadn't set her sights too high. He saw her subterfuge and cut through it, despite the fact she'd become a master at it. He let her go.

When one of the servers came near, she signalled for a glass of wine. She was going to need the fortification. She had no problem at all promoting others or her firm. But exposing her secrets? That required courage.

She took a long drink of her wine, then gripped the stem as if it were a lifeline. "I didn't know I liked kink until one of my boyfriends blindfolded me."

"What did you like about the experience?"

Several Doms and subs moved into the living room, and she looked around nervously.

"Eyes on me," he instructed.

Damn. He was relentless. She caught a glimpse of what he might be like as a trainer, and it terrified her as much as it intrigued her.

"Or excuse yourself now."

She looked up from where she'd been staring into the depths of her wine.

He missed nothing.

"I liked that I had no idea what would happen next. My hearing seemed heightened. And when he touched me, the sensation was magnified."

"Go on."

"One guy would sometimes swat my bottom when I passed him." She had no idea this would be so embarrassing. There was nothing sexual about the conversation, rather, the facts were somewhat clinical. But that didn't stop her from blushing. "Last Halloween, I attended a BDSM party. Compared to this..." She swept her hand around. The gathering at Master Damien's house was for people who lived the lifestyle. "Well, most of us were just dabbling. We wore outfits we bought at the costume store, but afterwards my date tied me up for the first time. It was just to his bed, and he used a light whip on my ass. I liked it. Well, enough to explore more. I wanted more experiences, but he said it really hadn't worked for him all that well. He didn't like hurting me. Even though I promised him he hadn't."

"You're telling me most vanilla guys aren't interested in spanking an ass like that?"

She blinked.

"I noticed you when you first came in, and you wore that skirt hoping I would."

"Yes," she admitted. "I did." It was one size smaller than she bought for business meetings, and she'd never wear it out in public. The material hugged her rear so tight she was nervous about sitting down.

"So show me."

"I beg your pardon?"

"Lift your skirt to your waist, turn around, spread your legs as far as you can, then bend over and grab your ankles."

For a moment she could hardly breathe. He said nothing further, and he looked unconcerned, as if it didn't matter to him one way or another whether she did as he said. She recognised it as a test, though.

He extended his hand to accept her glass. That was probably for the best—she was suddenly afraid of dropping it. He slid the stem onto the mantelpiece, then used his thumb to tip back his cowboy hat.

She pulled up her skirt, and she was grateful she'd worn a thong. Exposing herself to a stranger was far different than playing with a man she'd been dating.

Master Alexander continued to say nothing. She realised then that he was a man of few words, and he didn't repeat himself. There was no cajoling from him, no teasing, no 'Oh, come on, Chelsea, have a little fun'. This man was a Dom, not a play toy.

She turned away from him and followed the rest of his instructions. For at least sixty interminable seconds, he said nothing. Her heart beat faster. The tops of her shoes dug into her ankles, and blood rushed to her head.

"This is the ass you've had a difficult time convincing men to spank?"

"Yes," she said. Then she wondered what the protocol was for addressing him. Sir? Mr Monahan? Master? Alex? Alexander?

He caressed both her butt cheeks.

Slowly she began to relax.

Other people continued to move through the rooms, and one stopped to talk to him. He removed one hand and continued to rub her with the other.

She started to stand, but he pinched her upper thigh. She gritted her teeth and had to remind herself to stay in position rather than stand, drop her skirt and get the hell away from him.

Determination drove her. She'd worked two jobs through college, and she kept her eyes on the goal, even when she was exhausted. And she wanted Master Alexander to train her.

She tightened her grip on her ankles. Never in her twenty-nine years had she been more humiliated than she was right now. People at parties wanted to meet her, to brainstorm. She'd never been completely ignored, bent over, with her rear exposed.

Finally the man moved off. Although he kept one hand on her bare butt, Master Alexander said nothing. Chelsea didn't know what the hell to do.

Suddenly he slapped her left butt cheek, hard. She cried out, more from shock than because it had hurt. She wanted to stand, but she forced herself to remain in position.

"You may pull your skirt down and face me."

Her legs quivered as she stood. In the last three minutes, she'd had a bigger taste of BDSM than she'd had in the last six months. She wasn't sure she liked it.

"Tell me about your thoughts while you were bent over," he said when she was facing him again.

"I felt nervous and exposed."

"And how did you feel when I smacked you?"

"I was startled, I suppose. And I didn't like how impersonal your touch was. I could have been anyone."

"Was it difficult for you to remain in position?"

She reached for her glass of wine and took a deep drink. "Yes."

"Tell me why."

"I didn't know this would be an exploration into my psyche," she told him.

"Anyone who engages in BDSM with me opens every part of themselves—emotions, mind, thought process. It's your choice," he said. "You're free to leave at any time."

She rarely shared her innermost thoughts with anyone, not even close friends. But maybe because he was a stranger it might be easier. "I'm accustomed to being the centre of attention. I don't like to be left out. You ignoring me like that frankly pissed me off."

"But you stayed in position. Why?"

"Because I want you to train me. And I wanted to show you I can do it."

"Very good. By the way, you have a very spankable ass. It turned bright red with my handprint."

She wondered if the colour matched her face.

"Being a submissive is very different from being tied up, wearing a blindfold, or even getting a beating. What you just experienced is a sample of what you can expect as a sub. Doms typically adore and cherish their subs. Some couples, as you may have ascertained, indulge like you and your previous boyfriends, just with a few more rules and a bit more regularity. They may even use the words Dominant and submissive. To me, submission comes with strict protocols, with service, with attention to refined body movements. Do you have any idea what you really meant when you asked me to train you?"

"Maybe I didn't," she admitted reluctantly. She shrugged. "What you just showed me... I wasn't thinking it would be that hard core."

"Tell me what you mean by that."

"The whole being submissive thing..." She gnawed her lower lip. Once she realised she was doing it, she stopped immediately. Her mother had been harping on her about that her entire life. "I guess I thought it was mostly about getting spankings and being tied up."

"It's more a state of mind," he informed her. "What you're talking about falls under the broad umbrella of bondage and discipline. And it could just be added kink in an otherwise vanilla relationship. But submission is about putting someone else's needs before your own. And you do it from a genuine desire to serve, not because you see it as a means to an end. Most of all, it's about mutual trust."

She felt as if she'd been chastised.

"I appreciate your honesty," he said. "I'm sure we can find you a man to spank you."

She laughed nervously. "I don't suppose you'd be interested? I mean, it is your birthday, and someone should get a spanking, and I'm guessing you won't be baring your butt."

"Quite correct."

She wished he'd tip the cowboy hat back so she could see his eyes better. "You could consider it a birthday present," she suggested.

"I'm not all that interested in giving you a spanking. And it has nothing to do with your delectable derrière. I prefer subs who have a desire to serve. Within that context, a spanking for punishment is fine, and so is an erotic beating."

While she hadn't liked being ignored, or the nasty little pinch, she had liked his firm command and the way he'd so masterfully swatted her. It had stung. But the memory of it was making her horny. "I wish you'd reconsider," she said, hoping she didn't sound as desperate as she felt. "I can do anything I set my mind to. You won't be disappointed in me. I promise you that."

Just then, Master Damien called for everyone's attention.

Sara had told Chelsea that the man could have been a movie star. He had long, dark hair that was secured at his nape. Leather pants highlighted his strong muscles, and a short-sleeved black T-shirt revealed a tattoo she couldn't quite make out.

Some Doms and Dommes urged their subs to their knees for the announcement. Those instructed verbally or through hand commands knelt without complaint. She understood what he was trying to say. No one appeared to rebel against the indignity the way she instinctively had.

"We're celebrating Master Alexander's birthday tonight," Master Damien said. He nodded to a server, and the woman pushed a rolling cart into the living room. A half-sheet cake was ablaze with dozens of candles. He began to sing the birthday song — too bad Master Evan C wasn't in the room — and others joined in.

As everyone applauded, Master Alexander blew out the candles. And because she figured he wouldn't make a wish, she did.

"Chelsea will be helping to serve the cake," Master Alexander announced.

She frowned at him.

"Let's see how much you really want to be a sub," he said, looking at her.

She sucked at cake cutting. She could never get the pieces to stand up, and she always ended up with frosting all over her hands.

"Try it with a smile," he added.

The woman who'd wheeled in the cake offered her a huge knife. As Chelsea accepted the pearlescent handle, the other woman disposed of the candles. The same man who'd brought her wine earlier carried over a stack of plates.

After cutting some mostly straight lines, she picked up the cake spatula and transferred the corner piece onto a plate.

"Take it to Master Alexander," the woman advised.

Right. Chelsea was supposed to wait on him since he was the birthday boy. She picked up a plate.

"Don't forget the fork and a napkin."

She took the plate to him, and she hid her snarl behind a smile.

"Try again," he said.

"Excuse me?"

"Watch." He gestured to the woman server.

As she moved towards Master Damien, she kept her head tipped. She extended the plate and, when he accepted, she offered the fork and napkin as one package.

Chelsea scowled. She'd never noticed all that before.

"Keep watching."

The woman gave a brief, barely noticeable curtsy.

"Seriously? You expect me to do *that?*"

"You would receive this kind of instruction as part of your training."

Cheeks burning with humiliation, she carried the plate back.

Now that Masters Damien and Alexander had been taken care of, the help began to offer cake to the rest of the guests.

A bald man, apparently of some sort of Mediterranean heritage, was standing near the tray, arms folded across his chest. His shoulders and chest were massive, and she wouldn't have been surprised to learn he played professional football. Or maybe he made a living as a bouncer.

"No one is paying any attention to you."

"I beg your pardon?"

"Almost everyone here is with a sub, or they've been around the lifestyle for years. All subs have their behaviour corrected from time to time. It's totally natural." He smiled and set her at ease. "I'm Gregorio," he said. "I work with Master Damien here, and I take care of the Den. It's my job to ensure everything runs smooth."

"And that includes reassuring wannabe subs?"

His silver earring winked in the overhead light. "My jobs are many and varied."

"I'm not even his sub. I just want him to train me."

"So he's seeing if you're worth the effort?"

"He turned me down."

"Obviously, he's intrigued. You found a way to get an invite to a private party to meet him. Don't give up easily, unless you've decided it's not for you. In that case, move on and find someone who shares your kink."

She nodded.

"Are you planning to take the cake back to him?"

After thinking about it for a few seconds, she softly sighed and said, "Yes."

"Are you right-handed?"

"I am."

"In that case, I recommend you carry the plate in your left hand. Wrap the napkin around the fork and carry those in your right hand. Keep your head down, gaze lowered. At this point, he won't be expecting you to kneel. Concentrate on the pleasure he will receive from your service. Offer the fork and napkin first, and then seamlessly transfer the plate to your right hand so you have no awkwardness. The most important thing with service is to think about things ahead of time, plan them out, but have the room to be flexible if your Dom desires it."

"What about that little bow thing?"

"You can manage something, I'm sure. Bonus points if you use the term Sir or Master Alexander when you address him."

"Right now, I'm not sure I can remember my own name."

"That's why you need to concentrate on him, not yourself. Don't overthink," he added. "Try to be natural. You will screw up. Everyone does. Just accept the correction without taking it personally. As I'm sure Master Alexander has already advised, give yourself over to the experience of pleasing your Dom. Get out of your own way, allow someone else be the centre of your universe. If you're a submissive, you'll be fulfilled from pleasing him. It's not for everyone. It's not for most people."

Before she could thank him, he had moved off. Surreptitiously she watched another server. Cake was offered one way to Doms, and a little less formally to subs. Some Doms ate and refused a piece on behalf of their sub. One server was directed to place a plate on the floor for a sub. And as Gregorio had said, no one seemed to notice. The blonde sub held her hair back from face and began to eat. Her Domme placed the spiked heel of her boot on the girl's shoulder while she ate her own dessert.

Everyone had been telling her the same thing. Submission wasn't for everyone. The more she saw, the more she questioned the path she'd set for herself. Other people seemed to think this was normal, when it seemed anything but to her.

But then Master Evan C entered the room, electrifying it with his energy. The woman he'd been to the dungeon with looked beautiful with her smile and tracks from tears staining her cheeks. She walked over to the tray and carefully selected a plate for him. If others could find pleasure in this, so could Chelsea.

Doubly resolved, she straightened her spine and moved back towards Master Alexander, her gaze cast downwards. She focused on the act of serving him, ignoring the little voice protesting what she was doing. "Happy birthday, Sir," she said, following Gregorio's directions.

"Thank you," he replied. "But I've changed my mind about having cake."

She bit back her instinctive curse. "Of course, Sir."

"I've decided I'd rather give you a birthday spanking."

Chapter Two

"We need to get a few formalities out of the way," Alex told her once she returned to him. He thumbed back his hat and looked down at her. He'd been impressed by her reaction when he'd refused the plate. She'd blinked, and she'd given a small sigh, but she hadn't protested. Her behaviour hadn't been exemplary, but for a neophyte, it wasn't awful.

Now, she stood in front of him, a little farther away than he would normally permit, but he understood that his words had shocked her and she needed to keep a bit of a physical distance between them. He continued, "For the moment, I want you to look at me as we're talking. I want to be very sure you understand what I'm telling you."

Part of him wondered what the hell he was thinking. He'd stopped training over two years ago. Even when he'd done a fair amount of it, he'd only worked with subs who already had prior experience. He'd only been approached by a sub one other time. In her heart, her soul, every part of her being, Liz had said she was committed to the lifestyle, but she'd really been more of a masochist. Training had been a constant, and wearing, battle. She hadn't just wanted to be the perfect sub, she'd wanted to be beaten. The harder, the better. Though he'd fallen in love with her, her constant misbehaviour had devoured their relationship. There was never a time she hadn't been goading him.

The dissolution of their bond had devastated him, and in the past two years, he'd been selective with whom he'd played. He took no one home, and he formed no physical or emotional attachments. Not that he would have had the time, even if he'd had the inclination.

Chelsea had mentioned the Bartholomew scandal. And sometimes it seemed that everyone who lived in North America had heard of it. He, Gavin and their team had given months of due diligence. But one of their employees had overlooked some accounting irregularities, leading to devastating results for Monahan's clients.

Damien, a friend for years, and one of the investors who had lost big in the scandal, had organised Alex's birthday party and presented it as a fait accompli. He had insisted there were no hard feelings. Business was business. Sometimes a deal went south.

Now that he'd met Chelsea, he was grateful for his friend's generosity and glad to be back at the Den after an eighteen-month absence.

She was refreshing. Bold. Brazen. Unable to comprehend the word no. She made him forget his problems, and he knew time with her was exactly what he needed.

In general, he liked women with a few more curves than she had. He preferred longer hair. And he demanded more honesty and respect. But he admired her bravado.

She was at least five foot seven, even taller with the heels on. Her short blonde hair had chunks of dark highlighting, and the few curls that had escaped their clips lay on her forehead. But her green eyes snared and kept his interest. They were wide and expressive, and he could see her emotions revealed there.

The way she sometimes worried her lower lip charmed him. In the time they'd been talking, she'd worked off most of her lipstick, making her appear vulnerable. He doubted she'd appreciate that observation.

Although he had no intention of seeing her again past tonight, he could give her a taste of what she was really in for if she pursued her course of action. He understood why she'd want Evan C as a client, but frankly he thought the self-absorbed rocker was a wannabe and never-gonnabe. Evan C lacked discipline and vision, though he demanded that of the subs he played with. Still, the man had natural talent and, Alex supposed, that could sustain him as a cover band for some time.

But if Chelsea thought getting a little instruction would help her capture and keep Evan C's interest, she was wrong.

Subs were born, not made, and he'd observed her internal struggle when she'd served him cake, then he'd irritated and confused her when he'd refused her offering. She sure as sunrise hadn't appreciated being bent over, her pert rear exposed to the world, while he greeted guests. He saw her commitment, but his money was on her failing, no matter who she found to train her. She might enjoy whips, bondage and blindfolds, but subjugating her will would be a challenge, if not impossible.

Now that the formalities were out of the way, the party began in earnest. Evan C and his band moved into the sunroom and picked up the instruments that had been set up earlier. People spilled out onto the patios. One had a fire burning in a brick pit, another was warmed by several kerosene heaters. Several people headed for the dungeon. And that left him all but alone in the living room with the headstrong Chelsea Barton.

"You mean you've changed your mind about training me?" she asked.

"No." He shook his head. "I've decided to let you be my birthday present for the evening, if you're agreeable."

She sucked her lower lip between her teeth again. "Just know that I'll be trying to change your mind. I will want to spend real time with you learning how to please a Dom."

He grinned. "And I'll be trying to convince you to give up your quest. You're not a sub. Tonight will prove it."

She stuck out her hand.

The gesture startled him, but he accepted. They shook hands, and he noticed she once again had a determined tilt to her chin. They hadn't known each other an hour, but he was already familiar with it. *Game on.* He released her. "First of all, you will address me as Sir. You may call me Master Alexander, but not Master."

"What's wrong with calling you Master?"

"It's too confusing for someone as new as you. I'm not your Master. That speaks to a level of relationship we don't have."

"I think you underestimate me."

"Maybe," he conceded. "But that's part of being a good sub."

She scowled. "What is?"

"Following my rules, whether you like them or not, whether you agree with them or not."

"So I have to do everything you want?"

"Of course."

She swallowed deeply.

"Within reason," he amended. "We'll use a safe word, and I need to be aware of your limits."

"I really don't know much about my limits," she admitted, still looking up at him. "No permanent scars or markings, I suppose."

He respected that she hadn't looked away. "Understood. We'll learn about the rest of your limits together, then, through your safe word. Do you have one?"

"Parsley."

He raised his eyebrows.

"I hate the stuff."

"And you'll remember that during distress?"

"I remember to request it be left off my plate when I go out to eat. So yes, I'll remember."

"If it works for you, we'll use the word 'slow' if things are too much and you need a break."

She nodded.

"The Den also has a safe word. Halt. Master Damien, Gregorio, or any guest will intervene if you use that word. Are you clear?"

"Yes."

"Yes, Sir. Or yes, Master Alexander. From this moment forward, we are no longer equals, you and I. I am the Dom. You are the sub."

She took a little breath. "Yes, Sir."

"Now, about my birthday spanking…"

"Yes? Yes, Sir?"

"Let's go to the dungeon." He pointed towards the stairs. "After you."

Chelsea grabbed her wine, and he closed his hand around her wrist.

"Sober, or not at all," he told her.

She hesitated, then nodded. He released her and her hand shook as she returned the glass to the mantel. Their gazes met, and she looked away first.

She moved cautiously down the stairs, likely gripping the banister as much for balance as to settle her nerves.

Speakers blasted Evan C's music through the space. Lighting was dim, and the conversation was loud to compete with the band. "Give me your wrist," he said.

She frowned, as if not understanding the instruction, but offered her right hand. Since his last visit, several hooks had been attached to the walls. He'd heard a rumour that Damien had had them installed after one sub expressed shock that the dungeon didn't have shackles. Of course, Damien had said, a slave should be able to be chained to the walls.

Alexander used a thoughtfully provided leather strap to attach her to the hook.

"I…"

He spoke into her ear. "Obviously you can undo that as I only secured one of your hands." It would take her some time to unfasten it with her left hand, but it was doable if she panicked. "But I'd prefer if you remain where I want you while I go to the bar." He knew it would be easier for her if he remained standing near her.

"I'm the only one tied up like this."

"Yes," he said. "You are." He noticed she drew her eyebrows together and wondered if she was going to protest. "You're being a good girl."

"You know I find that a bit insulting."

"I'm sorry to hear that." But he wasn't surprised she felt that way. "It's not meant to be anything but an expression of my approval. Until you can see that, you'll never be a good sub. If you prefer, I could attach you to the wall by your neck. In fact..."

"This is fine, Sir."

"You may want to thank me for my kindness."

"Oh, God. I mean... Thank you, Sir."

That he had to coach her to use her manners for something so monumental informed him how unschooled she really was.

He kept a surreptitious eye on her as he ordered two bottles of water from the bar. A waiter carrying a tray of wine walked past her, ignoring her completely. He saw her pull against the tether in obvious consternation.

Rather than engaging in conversation with other Doms, he returned to her immediately. "When you're better trained, things like that won't bother you," he promised. "Again, concentrate on what pleases your Dom. I tied you to the wall because I wanted to, not because you were being punished. What would the experience be like if you had just centred yourself and thought about my imminent return?"

"This is difficult, Sir."

"You may safe word at any time and admit I was right."

"Hard doesn't mean impossible, Sir."

"In that case, next time I'll place you naked in the stocks. I understand they're portable and can be moved to the middle of the room. Completely adjustable so I can have you standing, sitting, kneeling, bent over, or even squatting. Depends on what part of your body I want exposed."

Colour drained from her face.

"And you'll thank me for the experience," he told her. "In fact, your lack of gratitude is a bit off-putting."

"I think I'm confused," she said.

"My time is valuable. Especially since it's my birthday, I would think I could find someone a little more agreeable to play with." One of the female servers, dressed in an apron and nothing else, was standing near the bar, looking over the space to see if she might be needed. He signalled to her, and she hurried over. Though she moved with purpose and speed, her motions were graceful.

"Sir?" she asked. "May I be of service?"

She had a purple band on her wrist. At the Den, this indicated she was a submissive. He knew that Damien often hired professionals to attend his parties. Unattached Doms enjoyed knowing they'd have someone to scene with. "Are you available for a short demonstration?"

"Of course, Sir."

"Do you have a safe word?"

"Red, Sir."

"Anything else I need to know about you…Brandy, is it?"

She smiled. "Thank you for remembering, Sir. Nothing else you need to know."

"Any issues with corporal punishment?"

"No, Sir."

He turned back to Chelsea. "Observe. Relax. This isn't about me pointing out your shortcomings, it's simply a part of your instruction."

Her lips were set in a tight line, but she said nothing.

"Remove your apron," he said to Brandy.

Within moments, she stood in front of him, naked.

"Please present your breasts."

Brandy cupped the abundant globes in her palms. She lifted her breasts and drew them together.

"Thank you," he said. "I'm going to squeeze your nipples extraordinarily hard."

"Of course, Sir."

He gave her a couple of gentle squeezes, preparing her for what was coming. When she leaned towards him, wordlessly indicating she was ready for more, he increased the pressure. She moaned. He backed off.

She exhaled. "Thank you, Sir."

He repeated the process, but this time he added more pressure.

Brandy closed her eyes and made noises that sounded like a soft purr.

When he withdrew, she kept her eyes closed. From her position, it was obvious she liked what he was doing and wanted more. Still, moments later, she opened her eyes again and said, "I appreciate your attentions, Sir."

"You're very welcome," he told her. He looked back at Chelsea. Her gaze was transfixed on Brandy.

"That had to hurt," Chelsea said.

Brandy looked at him for approval. After he nodded, she answered Chelsea. "It did. But Master Alexander knows what he is doing. He stopped before it became too uncomfortable, and I am aroused, and I know I can take more. I always thank a Dom for his attention."

Gregorio walked over to them.

"Kneel," Alex instructed Brandy.

The woman knelt gracefully, her legs spread wide, and she rested her bare buttocks on her calves. He preferred a slightly different stance, and before sunrise, he'd teach Chelsea several positions.

The difference in the two women was remarkable. Brandy turned her palms up, cast her gaze down, and drew long, deep breaths. Although she seemed at ease, he knew she was ready to respond to any command, no matter how subtle.

Chelsea was a different story. She was straining against the strap so hard he was afraid she was going to bruise. Though she looked at the floor as he spoke to Gregorio, she kept glancing back up. Alex understood her confusion. Earlier she'd been talking to Gregorio as an equal. The man was a switch, meaning he could sub or he could dominate. He related to subs and often helped them navigate their way through unfamiliar situations, but he wielded a wicked single tail, gave demonstrations, was an expert rigger, and the few times he'd been in relationships, he'd clearly been in charge.

What she needed to learn was that unless Alex said otherwise, she was to act as a sub to everyone. "Brandy, get on all fours and show your asshole to Gregorio."

"Of course, Sir." She placed her forehead on the cold tile floor, arched her back, and reached back to spread her buttocks.

He and Gregorio continued their conversation, ignoring both women.

Finally, the other man excused himself.

"Very nice, Brandy. Thank you for your assistance. You may get up and dress."

"Thank you, Sir."

She donned the apron, then returned to her duties.

He faced Chelsea again. "That kind of behaviour, flawless service, is what I expect, what any Dom will expect, from you. Would you like to continue your lesson, or shall we have a drink and listen to some of Master Evan C's music?" He left her attached to the wall while she considered her options.

"I'd like to continue on, Sir."

He nodded. "Brave girl."

He waited, but she didn't protest that he'd called her girl. As he unfastened the metal buckle, he was forced to admit a grudging respect for her. She was either committed to her course, or she was incredibly stubborn. Either way, he'd expected her to run before now.

When he had been a trainer, he'd often waited weeks or a month before asking a sub to practise in public. Fighting emotions was more difficult when you weren't alone with your Dom. "As you heard, Gregorio said that we can use the second space down the hall on the left. Before we go, you need to know there's a screen for privacy, but there's no door. If you cry or scream, as you will, others may hear you." Evan's unintelligible music was still chipping the paint off the walls, so maybe her sounds would be muffled. "And others may walk by and see you. You will be naked. The humiliation you've experienced so far will be nothing compared to what you'll endure over the next hour or so."

She rubbed at her wrist, but she tipped her head back. "Would you like me to follow you, Sir?"

He grabbed their water bottles and started down the hall, not checking to see whether or not she followed. He entered their assigned space and moved towards the side wall. As he familiarised himself with the paraphernalia and apparatus, he said, "Please strip."

He didn't look over his shoulder to see if she complied. "Then kneel in the centre of the room. Some Doms will permit you to use a mat. I will not."

As always, Master Damien ensured each room in the dungeon was well-stocked. Damien was not only a gracious host, but a shrewd businessman — Alex knew a production company often filmed at the Den and on its surrounding acreage. Because of the contract Master Damien had signed, he was able to let others use the facilities at very little charge. A couple of rooms had themes, but this one was multi-purpose. A padded, massage-type table was off to one side. Hooks had been strategically attached, but he doubted he'd be using them this evening.

After placing the water bottles on a shelf, he opened drawers, set out a container of disinfectant wipes, tossed a condom on the counter, laid out several of pairs of surgical gloves, then pulled out a bottle of lube.

He looked at the few assorted floggers, spankers and other implements hanging on the wall. He heard her moving around as he selected a thick flogger, apparently crafted from deer hide. It should provide a nice thud, but nothing too intense for her virgin skin.

When he faced her, she was in the same position Brandy had been in earlier. Chelsea was even looking at the floor. Her skirt and shirt were folded precisely. If she had actually removed all her clothes, he would have been quite satisfied with her behaviour. "What instructions were you given, girl?"

She looked up. "To strip and to kneel, Sir."

"Do you understand the meaning of the word naked?"

"I..." She sighed and rolled her hands into tight fists.

He wasn't sure if she was apprehensive or whether she was frustrated with him. "Was your thong expensive?"

"No, Sir."

"No emotional attachment to it?"

She frowned. "Of course not, Sir."

"Good." He took out a pair of emergency scissors and approached her. He crouched in front of her and snipped the material. "And the bra?"

"I'm happy to remove it, Sir."

"You had the opportunity. You asked no questions, therefore I believed you understood the instructions. When I asked you to repeat them, you did, perfectly. So again, did the bra cost a week's salary?"

"No, Sir."

He moved behind her to release the hooks, then he squatted in front her of her again as he cut through the shoulder straps. The ruined scrap of lace fell to the floor, near her thong. He caught her chin. "Lesson learnt?"

"Yes, Sir," she said, eyes wide and unblinking. "When you tell me to strip that means I am to be naked."

"You have ten seconds to remove your shoes. Remain on your knees."

He stood and worked the pulleys on the wall that would lower an overhead hook. Then he took out a small stool that was stored in a corner. Once things were prepared, he returned to her. Her shoes were laid alongside her neatly folded pile of discarded clothing. "The position you are in is what I call kneeling back. It's a fairly comfortable position for a sub. But you should place your hands palms up on your thighs."

When she did, he added, "It's not my favourite. I prefer kneeling up."

He took a cane from the wall. She couldn't know that he didn't intend to punish her with it, but rather, he would use it to correct flaws in her posture. He didn't explain it to her. It was fine with him if she had some questions, even better if she had some concerns.

He tapped the rattan against his knee. "When I instruct you to kneel, you can assume it means I want you in the kneel up position. This means placing your hands behind your neck." When she did so, he added, "Spine straight, and no more resting on your calves. Thrust out your breasts. Keep your knees far apart. Farther." He tapped the insides of her thighs with the cane. "Even more." When he was satisfied, he nodded. "This makes it possible to punish your pussy if I desire."

"I... Yeah. Scared."

"No need to be. Yet."

"You're trying to terrify me, aren't you, Sir? I think a cane on the pussy might be on the limits list."

"It doesn't have to be wicked," he said. "Now stand so I can inspect your naked body."

She hesitated for a moment.

"Many Doms like to ensure their subs have complied with their grooming rules. And sometimes they simply enjoy touching while she or he is helpless to move. For others, it's simply a perfunctory part of the relationship."

Like most novice subs, she stood awkwardly, putting a hand down to steady herself.

"We'll try that again, shall we? This time, keep your hands behind your neck. Use your abdominal muscles. It's tricky with shoes on, but since you're barefoot, it's easier to find your balance." He forced her to rise and kneel ten times before she was a bit out of breath. The altitude had something to do with it, he was sure, but also, that kind of motion taxed the body. "If you want to hold a Dom's interest, you'll practise that a hundred times a day. With heels, without shoes, holding a tray, hands in various positions. Doms expect beautiful movements...poetry in motion."

"Yes, Sir."

"For a standing inspection, I require you to keep your head up, looking straight ahead. Of course, others have different expectations, but if you're with someone for the first time and no other orders have been issued, this is a fairly safe default position. Of course, that doesn't mean you won't be punished for your assumption. I'll show you a lying down variation after we're done here. Now, push your elbows out farther so that your breasts are more prominently displayed. Bring your shoulder blades together."

"More trips to the gym are in order," she observed.

"I have a tongue clamp if you can't keep your mouth shut."

She didn't respond.

He tapped the insides of her ankles with the rattan and she spread her legs wider in response. "Good. Now. I intend to inspect you. Your mental state matters here. You can see this as a humiliating exposure, or you can see it as part of the procedure, or you can know you're pleasing your Dom. You can even, I know, unimaginably, enjoy the experience. It's all up to you." He walked around her. "You have a lovely body, Chelsea. You may thank me for the compliment."

"Thank you, Sir."

"Nice tits. Not too big. Thick nipples."

She was silent for a moment and he tapped her forearm with the cane to prompt her.

"Thank you, Sir."

"Now I'm going to see about the responsiveness of your nipples."

She sucked in a little breath.

"Do you have sensitive nipples, girl?"

"Not overly so, Sir."

"Mind if I find out for myself?"

Her hesitation was so slight that he might have missed it had he not been watching her so carefully. "Please do, Sir."

Before cupping her breasts, he put down the cane. "Stay in position." He lifted her breasts slightly then tightened his grip on the firm flesh.

Her breathing increased, but she didn't protest.

He moved his hands to gently squeeze her nipples. Though her mouth parted slightly, she continued to look ahead. He released her, then did it again, slightly harder. He did the same thing three times. "Now your cunt." He used his left hand to part her labia, and he skimmed the inside of the tender flesh. "Many Doms will want you clean shaven there. If you were my sub, I'd use a pair of tweezers to get every stray hair that you missed."

She swallowed hard.

"Lucky for you, you're not my sub. Some Doms prefer that look." He stroked her clit, then slid a finger inside her. She was nicely damp, responsive. He moved behind her and swatted her rear on both sides with an upwards motion of his hand.

She lost her balance momentarily before immediately getting back into position.

After putting on a pair of surgical gloves, he said, "Open your mouth."

For a moment she looked so mutinous he was betting on her using her safe word. Finally, as he stood there waiting, she yielded. He found it interesting that many subs didn't protest him probing any other orifice, but they didn't like him sticking his fingers in their mouth. "Wider. I mean it," he added when she didn't comply. "Good. Now stick out your tongue." He grasped the end of her tongue and pulled on it.

After he released it, he ran his finger around the inside of her mouth. He did this part to reinforce the totality of submissiveness. Once he was finished with that part, he said, "Now get on all fours like Brandy did, forehead on the floor, part your ass cheeks."

"Sir..."

"You can use a safe word, or you can ask me to slow down so we can talk about it. Or you can get on with it. Stalling will try my patience, and you won't get the most out of this experience tonight. I'm sure you're aware that many Doms use all their sub's holes."

She took her time, but she complied with his request. He crossed to the counter and pumped a dollop of lube onto two fingers. "How much anal experience have you had?"

"Very little...maybe twice. And I've never had more than one finger up there, Sir."

"Until today," he amended, returning to her. He started slowly, inserting the tip of a finger and then pulling back. He did that several times, going a bit deeper each time. "Bear down," he advised. "Feel this ring of muscle?"

"Embarrassing," she said.

He was glad she couldn't see his smile. "No embarrassment needed. It's totally natural. Bearing down will make it easier for me to get past the muscle and you'll feel less pain."

Her legs quivered, probably as much from the strain as from a healthy dollop of fear, but she did as instructed. Soon he had two fingers inside her. "Well done," he said approvingly as he finished up and removed the gloves. He disposed of them as she situated herself. "Return to your previous standing position and tell me what you thought of your first inspection?"

She looked ahead but didn't meet his gaze. "I suppose it was okay, Sir. I did what you said, and tried not to feel humiliated. I didn't really like the mouth part for some reason, and having you up my ass wasn't as painful as I thought it might be."

"Do you recall my earlier conversation about gratitude? I've yet to hear your manners, girl."

She went still, as if oxygen had been sucked from the room.

The pounding from Evan's music suddenly ceased, leaving everything silent.

"I... *Christ.* I mean, thank you. Thank you, Sir."

"Being inspected like that is a privilege, girl."

"I'm not sure I understand, Sir."

"I'll give you a demonstration. And unless you want another after that, I suggest you remember your manners." He cupped her breasts harshly and squeezed mercilessly.

"Oh, God! I understand. I'm sorry, Sir!" she gasped. "Thank you! Thank you!"

"Much better. Now your nipples." He pinched quickly and hard, then released her.

"Argh," she said, tears welling in her eyes. "Thank you, Sir."

He repeated the process, using extraordinary pressure.

"Sir! Sir! Thank you."

He slapped her pussy sharply. "I should use a cane on this to reinforce the lesson."

"Thank you for your kindness."

He fingered her cunt without bringing her any pleasure. When she didn't thank him quickly enough, he slapped her again and a third time. "Open your mouth." He donned a new pair of gloves while she nervously watched and waited. This time he forced her mouth apart until he knew her jaw ached. He met and held her gaze. Her eyes were wide and unblinking, filled with remorse. The little sounds she made were of gratitude, and she drew shallow breaths through her nose.

"Now show me that ass." Because he'd already stretched her anus, and because her rear passage had already been lubed, he squirted only a small amount of gel onto his fingertips before entering her with no prior verbal warning. He stretched her wide, and quickly added a third finger. He fucked her several times as she whimpered her gratitude. "Now, girl, kneel back and think about the differences in those experiences and how thankful you are that I was so lenient with you the first time."

Chapter Three

Emotion, regret, resolve and the residual pain from his use overwhelmed her. Chelsea had begged him to train her, but she had to admit that he was right. She'd really had no idea what she'd been asking for. It was a long way from kink that made her giggle to...this.

She struggled into the position he'd said, fighting for breath as she placed her upturned hands on her thighs. He draped a blanket around her shoulders.

Chelsea knew then she'd never been with a true Dom before. She had watched Sara and Lyle together, and at the parties she'd attended she'd observed a couple of scenes. Even here, she'd seen interactions between servers and others, subs and Doms. And still, she hadn't understood. Even though she'd watched it with her own eyes, Chelsea hadn't realised how perfectly Brandy responded to Master Alexander. It was obvious she was focused on only him while she'd knelt, while she'd been exposed, while he'd brutalised her nipples.

When they'd talked, Gregorio had tried to explain it to Chelsea. But the last ten minutes had changed everything for her. She finally understood. Being a sub wasn't just about getting an occasional mind-blowing experience. It was about transcending or transforming your perceptions. Maybe the whips and chains were part of it, but they weren't all of it.

She took in a few breaths and blinked back the tears.

"Please look at me," Master Alexander said in a soft and reassuring voice. He didn't sound like the same person she'd just been with.

She glanced up. He stood there, holding an uncapped bottle of water.

Somewhere along the line, he'd removed the cowboy hat. Now that she saw his whole face, he looked even more implacable. His short, dark hair was swept back from his deeply lined forehead. His rich brown eyes were penetrating, as if they saw into her, past the outer façade that almost everyone, including her family, knew, and into the inner depths she revealed to no one.

"Drink some of this." He extended the bottle.

Her hand shook as she accepted. Several drops of water splashed over the side. After managing a few sips, she offered it back and swiped her hand across her mouth before resuming the correct position.

"Parsley?" he asked.

"No chance, Sir. I hate the stuff."

"There's no shame in stopping this," he said. "Many people find they want something lighter, that they're not cut out for anything other than an occasional scene. That's a perfectly viable option."

"Even if people rarely indulge, aren't there still expectations?"

"There are. But not all Doms are as firm as I am about inspections and impeccable service. As long as you're somewhat well behaved, you'll satisfy most people you play with."

"But right now I will not satisfy the most discerning Doms, Sir." *Like Master Evan C.*

"True. But not everyone expects perfection. Many people who play are satisfied with the illusion. They want to beat someone and get their cock sucked or pussy licked."

While they'd been talking, her heart rate had returned to normal. Sweat had dried on her body. And she'd mostly managed to corral her thoughts.

"So you want to continue on?"

"I may be a slow learner, Sir, but I am learning. You won't have to repeat that lesson. Yes, please, I'd like to continue on. Thank you for the water, and for the two inspection examples."

"If you had more experience, girl, I wouldn't have gone so easy on you."

"Easy, Sir?"

"It could have involved a cane, perhaps an oversized plug or dildo in your anus, clamps on your cunt to hold the labia apart, having your mouth opened with a dental gag and maybe being washed out with soap. You could have been manhandled considerably worse."

No doubt what he said was true. She shivered, despite the blanket. "Thank you, thank you, thank you for going easy on me, Sir."

"You still have the chance to back out."

"Thank you, Sir." She was resolved. She'd shown up here tonight hoping for exactly this. In her life she'd often found that things that seemed easy at first turned out to be more difficult than she could have imagined. But she'd also discovered the things she worked hardest for were the most rewarding in the end.

"In that case, lie down on that table for a supine inspection." He removed the blanket from her and said, "Hands at your sides. Feet flat on the surface about shoulder-width apart. Knees upraised. Some Doms may do this on the floor, or a bed, or a table top. A kitchen table is perfect if he or she has company."

She blinked. For some reason, when she thought of this, she assumed the Dom would be male.

"It can be enjoyable to either watch someone else use the sub or to have others see him do the inspection. A bit of voyeurism. For now, we'll keep it between us."

"Thank you, Sir."

This time she knew what to expect, so that had to make things easier.

As she'd seen Brandy do, Chelsea took a few deep breaths to centre herself. It surprised her that she was able to relax while knowing he was watching.

Master Alexander squeezed and kneaded her breasts and she moaned. Instead of releasing her, he changed his grip so that he could flatten her nipples between his thumb and forefinger. It felt as if he'd trapped her in a vice. "Thank you, Sir," she whispered. Knowing what to expect hadn't made it easier. Even though he was doing essentially the same things, he was doing them differently. He was studying her reactions, keeping her gaze ensnared. And, heaven help her, his touch was a bit more sensual and she was becoming aroused.

"Very nice nipples."

"Thank you, Sir."

"How high can I tug them before you beg for mercy?"

"Is this part of an inspection, Sir?"

"Certainly, girl. Gauging your responses, capabilities and obedience is the biggest part of it."

"Thank you for explaining that, Sir."

"I'm going to pull up your nipples. Keep your legs apart and your feet flat. Understand?"

"Yes, Sir."

"Feel free to cry or whimper or moan. Screaming is okay, too. But when you absolutely can't take any more, say slow. But take as much as you can."

"Yes, Sir."

His grip was excruciating. But then he began to pull, as well.

She curled her hands into fists. He tugged a bit more and kept looking at her. She could drown in the depths of his eyes. And suddenly this wasn't all about her. She wanted to please him.

She was tempted to close her eyes from the ever-increasing pain, but looking at him gave her strength.

"Can you take more for me?"

She gritted her teeth. Since she'd met him, everything had been a battle of wills, and she had no intention of losing. "Of course, Sir."

Her abdominal muscles constricted and drawing a breath was difficult.

"Good girl."

This time he sounded approving, rather than patronising. She wondered if his tone had changed or if her attitude had.

He pulled harder and she dug her heels into the table cushion. The amount of pain she was enduring wasn't possible. As the agony increased, she became more turned on.

"That exquisite line between pain and pleasure," he told her. "You're there. Endorphins and horniness. I can smell you."

Yes. She was. She wanted…something.

He pulled a little harder and she squeezed her eyes shut and cried out, "Slow."

"Well done," he said. "I'm going to release you a bit at a time so it hurts less."

"Thank you," she said, while desperately wishing he'd just let the hell go. Still, when he finally did, she cried out. The feeling of the blood rushing back into the abused tips, restoring them to their usual plumpness, was awful.

"Now I know where this limit is so I can, with your permission, push you further in future."

She wasn't sure anyone was going near her nipples again. Ever.

"Stay in position."

She opened her eyes in terror when he returned. He had several items with him, including a towel and more of those damn blue gloves, but the metal contraption that he held up riveted her attention.

"This is a dental gag."

It resembled a medieval torture device. It was quite wide with two metal pieces running parallel and a ratchet on either side, presumably to keep the teeth apart.

"As you can see, the bits are dipped in rubber, so it's quite safe. A lot of Doms like them because they restrict speech and keep the mouth open for insertion of a cock or a type of bladder."

"This is for educational purposes, right, Sir?"

"Instructional. Once it's inserted, and you get a feel for it, I'll remove it. When I inspected you earlier, I noticed how far you could comfortably open your jaw. Some subs find this kind of gag rather pleasant. They don't have to remember their manners and they can surrender to the scene. In lieu of a safe word, we'll use a safe signal. Simply raise your right hand and I'll remove it."

This man was pushing all of her boundaries. Never, even in her kinkiest thoughts or readings, had she imagined enduring anything like this.

"Open wide."

For a moment, she simply stared. She wasn't stalling, she was considering whether to stop him, this…madness.

"Chelsea, safe word or open your mouth."

Her fingernails gouging into her palms, she opened her mouth.

He began to adjust the ratchets, spreading her mouth apart. Just when fear clawed at her and she was ready to raise her hand, he stopped.

"I pay very close attention to you, girl. I know what you can take. I want you to breathe and accept the gag for about two minutes. It will feel like an interminable amount of time. But I will not leave your side."

He smoothed the hair back from her forehead. Even though the experience was freaky, she could trust him. And she knew right then that she would do as he asked.

"Fifteen seconds," he announced.

She was sure it had been four times that.

"You really are beautiful in your submission, Chelsea. There's something alluring about a woman who knows her power and isn't afraid of it. And when she surrenders it, it's magnificent. You doing okay?"

She nodded.

"Your shoulders are tense. Try to relax."

Her whole body was rigid.

"Uncurl your hands."

When she didn't, he simply took her left hand and opened it, very, very gently.

"You're still okay. Now try with the other."

Reluctantly she did.

"I promise, some subs find this experience sublime. It's easier to let go when you're not required to speak. You've got a minute left. Give up the struggle. Match my breathing."

He continued to hold her hand. She looked at him. The man was both her salvation and damnation.

"That's it. Breathe with me."

As she stopped fighting the experience, she realised it didn't hurt her jaw. She was still communicating with him. And she'd never felt more attuned to another human being.

"Good," he said. "Time's up." He pulled away his hand. "You should be proud of yourself. I'm just going to give you a quick demonstration of how an oral inspection might work with the dam in place."

She nodded again.

"It would probably be a little farther open, but I won't do that at this time." He inserted his gloved finger into her mouth. He felt around the inside of her lips, pushed on her teeth, pressed against the inside of her cheeks.

"Makes you very much aware of giving up control, doesn't it?"

It did. He was standing above her, totally in control, large, uncompromising, a Dom sure of his power and unafraid to use it.

He overwhelmed her.

"You can imagine how this probe could be much more degrading and uncomfortable."

She blinked.

"This, Chelsea, is submission." He removed the dam and wiped her mouth with the towel. "No worse for wear?"

She wasn't able to find her voice, so she shook her head and hoped she wouldn't be in trouble. He helped her sit. She flexed her jaw and then took a couple of grateful sips of water before thanking him for the experience. The other times, gratitude had come easier than it did now.

Once she had regained her equilibrium, he helped her to lie down and he resumed his inspection. This time he pulled back the hood of her clitoris to play with the nub. Most men she'd been with only had a passing acquaintance with her clit, but he plumped it, tweaked it, stroked it, fondled it then, making her scream, licked it. She grabbed the table and lewdly pushed her pussy into his face.

"You have a very responsive body," he said, moving on.

"Thank you, Sir."

He inserted one finger inside her. "Your G-spot should be about..." He felt around a bit. "Here."

She arched and struggled, wanting more, wanting him to stop.

"Do you want an orgasm, girl?"

"Yes! Yes, please, Sir."

He continued his relentless motions. She was on the edge. The treatment of her nipples, the crashing emotion that the surrender to his gag had caused, then the way he touched her clit, the way her ass had been stretched wider than ever before, and now...heaven help her, he slipped a second finger into her cunt and pressed his thumb to her anus... "Sir!" She thrashed her head about. In this moment, he owned her reactions. "Please." She panted. "I need... I can't, I can't." Her legs shook. "Please, slow..."

"Come."

To ensure her compliance, he licked her cunt as he fucked her pussy and used the thumb of his other hand to fuck her ass.

She had never had a man command her to orgasm, but she came, hard, fast, completely, screaming his name. Her entire body shuddered with the effect.

When the world stopped spinning, he was standing, one hand on top of her head. He stroked her cheekbone.

"Thank you, Sir." She assumed she was supposed to thank him for the orgasm.

"If I were training you, we would work on orgasm control."

"Yes, Sir," she lied. Flat-out lied. It didn't matter if she hired him or not. She would never deny herself that kind of experience. Anytime she had the opportunity to come like that, she'd take it. It was worth any punishment he might devise. She'd never had a climax that rocked her toes.

He helped her into a sitting position, ordered her to drink another sip of water, then said, "If a sub passes inspection and the Dom doesn't need to punish her for something or have her correct something in her grooming, they move on to the next thing."

The next thing? There's more after that?

"For example, the Dom's birthday present."

"Of course, Sir."

"Assuming you still want to continue."

The more he goaded her, the more resolved she became. Even if she wasn't able to convince him to train her, the things she'd already learnt would help her attract Master Evan C's attentions. "Yes, Sir."

"Have you ever played with a flogger?"

"At the parties I attended, yes. But I'm betting it was nothing like you mean."

She watched as he moved a small stool to the middle of the floor. Then he went to the far wall and lowered a pulley. It didn't take her long to add up the facts. She was going to be standing on the stool and attached to the hook. As she'd guessed, this was nothing like the playtime she'd had with others.

Her nerves skittered when he removed his bolo tie and hung it on the wall. His vest and shirt followed, and when he turned back towards her, she was even more aware of him as a man and as a formidable Dom. His chest was broad, and his biceps well defined. He had a small amount of dark chest hair that gave him a sexy edge. When she had fantasies, this was the type of guy who showed up centre stage.

She vehemently disagreed with the little voice suddenly nagging her, informing her that he, rather than Evan C, was the right kind of man for her. Master Alexander was too brash and demanding. Besides, she definitely wasn't the type of woman he would be attracted to.

He helped her from the table. For a moment she was close, far too close, to his chest, to being in his arms.

When he had been fully dressed, the atmosphere had felt somewhat instructional. Now sensuality simmered on the surface. He'd brought her to a rocking orgasm, and it wasn't just because of what he'd done to her body. It was because of the connection that arced between them. She liked the touch of his strong fingers on her skin. His commanding tone of voice made her want to bend her knees.

Music began to blare again, shattering the intimate air. She was grateful. It would be easy to forget she wanted to learn about submission so she could ensnare a different Dom.

"I'm going to bind your wrists together and then attach you to that hook."

He confirmed what she suspected, and she nodded bravely.

"I want you on your tiptoes, but I will do nothing that will compromise your safety."

"Meaning you won't dislocate my shoulder, Sir?"

He didn't bother responding to that. "Since today is my thirty-third birthday and you graciously offered to accept my spanking on my behalf, I'm going to flog you thirty-three times. No part of you is off-limits."

"I'm not sure what you mean by that, Sir."

"This is a fairly lightweight implement, meant for beginners. You'll feel an impact, for sure, but it won't cut or sting overly much. I intend to whip your entire body, breasts, buttocks, thighs, calves, pussy, stomach."

"Yes, Sir."

He studied her for a moment before nodding. He selected a pair of cuffs — thankfully they were fabric, rather than metal — then fastened them around her wrists.

"Onto the stool," he said.

Filled with trepidation, she took the big step up.

Motions efficient, he attached the cuffs to the hook, then slowly hoisted her onto her toes. She was stretched farther than she ever had been before, and she felt the tension throughout her entire body.

"How's that?" he asked.

"Tolerable, Sir."

"Good." He double-checked all the rigging. "Parsley?"

"Sir is a dreamer." She expected the beating to begin immediately, but he shocked her by vigorously rubbing her legs, then her buttocks and arms. He used a much gentler pressure on her front, but he covered her entire body. "That's nice, Sir."

"You're welcome, sub."

He picked up a flogger, and it felt as if the room temperature dropped by at least ten degrees. It had been one thing to discuss it theoretically, another to have him approach with the wicked-looking strands dangling from his hand.

"Ready?"

She licked her lips. "Yes, Sir." She wasn't, but then she figured she probably never would be.

"We'll do the first fifteen on your back."

She willed him to get on with it.

The first landed on her buttocks. She inhaled sharply, but didn't protest. The anticipation had been worse than the actual hit.

He placed the second at the small of her back.

And then she was lost to the thuddy sensations. Back and forth, he caught her shoulders, her calves, her thighs, and the sensitive area beneath her ass cheeks. She jerked and occasionally cried out when he only caught her with the ends.

Then suddenly, he stopped. Was that fifteen?

"Your entire back is red," he told her. "It looks beautiful."

"Thank you, Sir."

"I'm glad you remembered your manners so we didn't have to begin again." He moved in front of her and shook out the strands. "Are you ready to continue?"

She nodded. Watching him was so different from having him behind her. Seeing his eyes narrow as he selected the spot he intended to strike was frightening. The man was more focused and intent than anyone she'd ever met.

When the strands connected with her belly, she closed her eyes. She was more relaxed when she wasn't able to see what was going on.

The strands bit at her breasts and curled around her sides. Her breathing became more and more laboured. She wasn't sure if he was hitting harder, or whether her front was more sensitive than her back, or maybe it was psychological.

"You're doing well," he told her. "You can do this. Relax your body. And your mind."

She opened her eyes. Earlier he'd mentioned that he was always watching her, and she now recognised how true that was. She could trust him.

"Thank you, Sir." She adjusted her stance and closed her eyes again.

This time, when he flogged her breasts, she didn't pull away.

"Good, girl," he said.

His words soothed rather than annoyed her. She liked the criss-cross caress of the leather strands, and she knew her nipples had hardened. Now she understood why some people talked about flogging euphorically.

"Open your eyes," he said. "I think the sub likes to be flogged."

"Are you finished, Sir?"

"Those fifteen are, yes."

"Oh. Thank you. You were right. I did enjoy that more than I thought possible."

"This wasn't a punishment," he said. "I assure you the flogger, especially crafted from something such as buffalo, feels quite different from this. The number of strands, their length and the way the Dom wields it changes the intensity, as well. Don't assume all beatings are like this."

"Yes, Sir. Thank you for clarifying that." She was getting the hang of the right verbiage. When he stood there, still flicking his wrist rather than letting her down, she frowned. Then she remembered. "You're thirty-three today, Sir." And he'd only hit her thirty times.

"Ask for your last three."

"May I have them on my breasts, Sir?"

"You may not. Spread your legs."

Goose bumps chased up her arms. He couldn't mean...

He stooped and moved her feet apart. *Now* she was frightened.

"Ask me to whip your cunt. Give me a birthday present to remember."

Her tongue felt too big for her mouth. But she also knew that drawing this out wouldn't help. "Please, Sir, whip my cunt."

"My pleasure, girl. And if you draw your thighs together, we'll start over until we get three good ones in a row. Are you clear?"

"Very clear, Sir." In anticipation, she pressed the balls of her feet harder against the wood.

The first shocked and seared. This was nothing like the ones he'd delivered to her breasts. The second was less painful, and the last was so gentle that her scorched clitoris started to demand attention. Her pussy throbbed.

He was a master all right, in every way. He'd turned her on with tails of leather.

"Happy birthday, Master Alexander," she said. "And thank you for giving me the gift."

"The gift was all mine," he told her. "I'm going to lower you, and when I do, I want you to move slowly."

Her body felt leaden, and she shrugged to restore circulation as soon as she was able. All the while, she looked at him. His body was beautifully hewn, and she wanted him. "Sir, this may be untoward, but would you fuck me?"

"It's not a good idea to confuse training that way."

"But you're not my trainer," she pointed out. And she wanted to be taken hard, by a man as uncompromising as he was. He knew her body better than she did. "Sir."

He unfastened her wrists. "Chelsea—"

"You're the one who made me horny, Sir."

"Get on the table."

"Yes, Sir," she whispered. She didn't smile until she was faced away from him. She perched on the edge of the table and studied him as he undressed.

Deliciously, he was commando beneath the jeans. His pubic hair was well trimmed, and his cock jutted out. She'd been so caught up in her own sensations that she hadn't seen how hard his cock was.

And what a gorgeous cock it was. Big, thick and pulsing. The sight of a man's penis had never made her salivate before. But then, she'd never wanted sex this badly, either.

"Lie down," he instructed while sheathing himself in a condom. "But keep your legs where they are. You're going to be wrapping them around my waist."

There would be no doubt he'd be fucking her, rather than making love. His way of keeping the demarcation line between what they had and a relationship? Regardless, it worked for her. She wanted it raw.

She lay back and spread her legs in invitation.

"Is your pussy hot, girl?"

It is now. His coarse language heightened the energy in her raging hormones.

He moistened his thumb pad and pressed it against her clit. She arched up, wordlessly begging for more. And he gave it to her, rubbing her gently, then harder, then backing off again. "Yes, please, Sir."

Instead of taking her to completion, he guided his cockhead towards her entrance. She wrapped her legs around him, as much for balance as anything, as he forcefully took her.

"Play with those pouty tits," he said. "I want to see your expression. Make sure you squeeze your nipples hard or I'll put a pair of clamps on them and yank on the chain so hard you'll see stars."

He drove into her. There was nothing sweet or reserved about his claiming. She gasped from the depth. "Damn, Sir."

"Is this what you wanted, girl?"

"It is!" It was. He filled her and satisfied the urge crawling through her veins.

"It's what I want, too," he said, his voice husky with pleasure. That he was so vocal about being turned on increased her arousal.

"Do me, Sir," she pleaded.

"My pleasure."

He thrust into her repeatedly, making her body jerk from the force. She played with her breasts and pinched her nipples. From the way he'd used her earlier, the tips were still swollen and sensitive, and that only heightened her need.

When she was on the verge of an orgasm, he stopped.

"Knees over my shoulders," he instructed.

Damn, how could he read her so well?

He helped her into the position he wanted. "Perfect," Master Alexander said. He leant forward, letting her body take his weight. It stretched her hamstrings unbelievably, and it permitted him in so deep she couldn't draw a full breath.

"Sir..."

"All of me, girl. Take all of me."

"Yes," she whispered.

He held her ankles tenderly, but pistoned his hips, and she screamed.

The discomfort of being impaled so forcefully made her come. She hadn't asked permission—she hadn't been capable of it. The climax had claimed her so hard and fast, she was helpless.

"Beautiful, my horny little cock slut," he said, but the words held no threat of retribution. "There's more." After he released the grip he'd had on her ankles, he brushed her hands aside and pinched her nipples as he continued to ride her.

"I apologise, Sir. I—" Her scream swallowed the rest of the words. The exquisite agony he inflicted, combined with the relentless, deep pounding, made her come again.

Chelsea was lost.

He groaned as he fucked her. It felt impossibly hard to her, and so very sexy. Their gazes collided and she saw raw desire there. Then he closed his eyes and gave a deep guttural moan. That she had that kind of power over him intoxicated her. As he ejaculated, his dick got bigger, and the penetration was deeper than ever. It hurt, but it felt good at the same time.

More considerate than any lover she'd been with, he released her breasts and played with her clit to bring her off one more time. She came so hard that she forced out his semi-hard penis.

"Stay there," he said.

As if she could move, even if he ordered her to.

Realising she was panting, she took a steadying breath.

He removed the condom and quickly cleaned up, then returned with a cool washcloth to soothe and cleanse her pussy. "Thank you, Sir." She'd never had a man do this before. And she liked it.

He offered his hand to help her up. "You've made this a memorable birthday. Thank you."

She was satiated. And more determined than ever to get this man to agree to train her. She just needed a plan.

Chapter Four

"Chelsea did what?" Alex asked, sitting back in his chair and looking out of the window towards the foothills. Damien's call had surprised Alex, but his gut-twisting reaction to the news stunned him.

"She called Niles," Damien repeated unnecessarily.

On the surface, that wasn't a bad idea. At one time, Niles had been as well-known as he was respected in the community. Since the death of his wife, he'd become reclusive. He participated in some scenes filmed at the Den, but he saw no one beyond professional models and actresses. Just like Alex, Niles had an edge to him. But Niles was rougher, more remote. Some wondered if he was capable of emotional attachment. Alex shoved away the unwelcome idea that the same description could apply to him.

"Niles turned her down," Damien continued. "But he gave her several recommendations."

She wouldn't be deterred. Alex should have realised that and not ended the evening the way he had, by wishing her well in her endeavours. She wanted to snag Evan C, and so would recklessly pursue any path that got her there. It didn't matter that he'd refused to train her, she would find someone, anyone who would. And not everyone could be trusted. Foolish girl. "Thanks for the heads-up," he said.

Before ending the call, he updated Damien on a couple of their investments, one that was doing as well as expected, one that was performing better than anticipated. They didn't make up for the colossal failure of the Bartholomew deal, but it was a start. He was pursuing other opportunities, but before he said anything, he and Gavin would be triple-checking all the details.

Alex slid his cell phone onto the desktop and stared at the sunset. At least this was one good thing about their recent move to the less expensive address. Their Cherry Creek offices had lacked the view that the Denver West area provided.

He thought about Chelsea, just like he had done every night this week. He'd enjoyed playing with her, introducing her to things she'd never tried before, seeing what made her nervous, then pushing her past those apprehensions.

Since Liz, he'd spent his nights alone. Until Chelsea, he'd had no desire to change that.

The idea of her going through all the Doms in Denver pissed him off. She could be hurt. And damn it, he wanted to be the one to watch her green eyes open wide, to soothe her brow when she was frightened, to teach her proper decorum. If she was so desperate to be trained, he would be the one to do it.

He picked up his phone and scrolled through the contacts list until he found the number for Sara's Dom. Within five minutes he had Chelsea on the line. "Round one to you."

"Excuse me?"

"You win," he conceded.

"Does this mean you're agreeable to training me?"

He heard excitement in her tone. Not just triumph, but honest enthusiasm. She might have won, but if she was gloating, she was disguising it well. "I'll give you two weeks. Are you available in the evenings and on the weekends?"

"There are a couple of events that I need to attend, but mostly I can rearrange my schedule, Sir."

"I recommend we start tomorrow."

"That works."

"Dinner? Six o'clock."

"That works," she said.

He named a restaurant near his office. "Wear a short skirt, heels, no undergarments. And pack an overnight bag in case you decide to stay. Any questions?"

There was silence. "How much will this cost me?"

"I don't charge."

"In that case, I'll make a charitable donation in the name of Monahan Capital."

He exhaled. She might not be a masochist like Liz had been, but that didn't mean he would have the patience he needed to deal with her annoying persistence. "Don't be late."

"Yes, Sir."

He half expected her to call and try to change the arrangements, and he was pleasantly surprised when she didn't. He arrived at the restaurant five minutes early, and she was already there. Impressive. She was sitting on a bench, her impossibly long legs crossed. Her back was hunched slightly, as if she were trying to hide the fact her breasts were bare beneath the loose-knit sweater. Her beauty was startling, and he was man enough to notice and appreciate it.

He'd prefer to see her present her body more proudly, and they'd be working on that. The next time they dined in public, her behaviour would be different.

With the artificial, calculating smile he recognised from the first time she approached him at the Den, she stood and offered her hand, as if he were a business associate. He ignored her hand and said, "I'd prefer you to kiss my cheek."

She blinked. "Of course," she said, leaning towards him.

"Of course, Sir," he corrected.

"Of course, Sir," she repeated, then kissed his cheek.

"Please," he said, indicating she should precede him. When she did, he placed his fingers as the small of her back. "Stand up straighter." He heard her draw a sharp breath, but she did so. "Reservations for Monahan," he told the hostess.

After they were seated, with menus in hand, he asked Chelsea, "Any preference?"

She looked at the entrées. "Probably just a salad. With sirloin. Maybe some wine."

"How do you like your steak cooked?"

Over the top of the menu, she scowled at him.

"I'll be ordering your food," he told her.

"I'm capable of doing that myself."

"Of course you are, but this is about your willingness to allow me to handle the details."

She put down the menu.

"A good Dom always takes his sub's desires into account. A good sub in turn trusts he will make good decisions on her behalf. If you have any preferences, now is a good time to express them."

"I don't like this," she admitted.

"Over the next two weeks, there will be plenty of things you don't like. You have a choice to deal with it or end your training."

She drummed her fingers on the table.

"This isn't as easy as you'd anticipated, is it?"

The waiter stopped by, and Alex ordered them each a glass of red wine. She set her chin mutinously, but said nothing.

"You may find my dominance irritating. Or you could decide it's nice to have someone take care of you for a change. It can be a struggle, or not. But understand this, bad behaviour will be corrected and perhaps punished. So, Chelsea, shall we proceed, or just have dinner as friends?"

"Do you expect me to address you as Sir, even in public?"

"When we are out as a Dom and sub, yes. If we were at a business event, that would be discussed and rules agreed to beforehand."

She was silent for so long he wasn't sure if she was going to answer. Finally she said, "I like my steak medium-rare, Sir."

He nodded. "Now sit up straight. I like that you dressed according to my desires."

"I am, Sir. It feels weird not wearing a bra."

"I like to see your nipples. And visualising them with clamps on."

She sipped from her water. "I'm not sure I've recovered from last weekend."

"Poor thing."

"I'm not hearing any sympathy, Sir."

"No. You're not." The waiter returned with the wine, and Alex ordered their meals and remembered to say, "Please ensure there is no parsley anywhere near the lady's plate."

The man nodded.

She smiled.

When they were alone again, Alex asked her, "Rather painless, wasn't it?"

"Yes, Sir. It wasn't nearly as bad as I'd made it in my mind."

"Did it take away from your empowerment?"

She sank against the back of her chair. "No." She picked up her wine. "It didn't change who I am, Sir, or the fact I'm capable of ordering my own food at any other time."

He nodded. "First lesson. Being submissive doesn't take away anything from you as a person or as a woman. You'll enjoy the meal you wanted, cooked the way you like, and you delighted me in the process."

"Yes, Sir."

"Not all Doms order for their subs, but many do. Take your lead from him, or her, and don't argue in the process."

"I understand," she said.

As they drank wine, she told him about her desire to succeed.

"My father abandoned us when I was ten. Mom forced me to go to college so that I wouldn't end up struggling like she had. She made sure I knew I couldn't count on anyone except myself." She toyed with her knife and fork. "She worked her ass off at two jobs so I could go to community college, then on to university."

"And taught you never to take no for an answer."

"True. It just means I need to find another way of asking the question," she said. "And you? When are you going to let me organise a charity function for Monahan Capital?"

"Do you ever give up?"

"Certainly, Sir." She smiled. "As soon as I get what I want."

He relaxed in his chair, watching her. That smile wasn't the hundred-watt fake one she usually gave him. This one was fun, impish, and it revealed a playful side of her that he hadn't known existed. He liked that she was more complex than he'd realised.

The waiter delivered their meals, and when he checked back to be sure everything was okay, Alex glanced at Chelsea.

"It's fabulous, Sir."

"Well done," he told her when the waiter left.

"You were right," she said. "Not just tonight, but the other night. If I think about what my Dom wants, the struggle isn't as difficult."

"Lesson two," he said. "At this rate, we'll be done in three days."

"Do you think so?" she asked, holding a fork poised near her mouth.

"No." He grinned when her shoulders fell again. "You're still slouching, despite the fact I've already corrected you twice."

She put down the fork and sat up. "Sorry, Sir."

"Not to worry, I have just the thing to help reinforce my will. I'll show you when we get to my house." He cut a piece of steak. "Eat up."

She left part of her salad and refused dessert and coffee. He paid the bill, and she protested. "If I want you to pay, I'll let you know. This changes nothing between us and takes nothing away from your feminine power. So give up the fight."

"In that case, thank you, Sir."

He nodded, wishing all arguments with her were this easy to end. "Did you bring an overnight bag?"

"I did. But I'd prefer not to stay, Sir."

"That's up to you. I have a guest room. And a chain at the end of my bed with a nice pile of blankets on the floor."

Colour drained from her face, and she pushed away her wineglass.

"Some Doms expect their subs to sleep on the floor."

As if choosing her words with great care, she asked, "Is that your expectation, Sir?"

"No." He'd had the chain installed for Liz when he'd trained her, and he'd done it at her request. He was happy to snuggle after a session, and there were nights when he wanted his woman to sleep in his arms. Liz had never wanted to do that. Even if he hadn't taken the time to chain her and arrange her bedding, he would wake up to find her on the floor, cocooned with her pillow and a single blanket, her collar affixed to the chain. "I had a sub once who preferred it that way. It helped her."

"I don't understand."

He wasn't certain why he was discussing this with her. "Liz was a masochist. Being in my bed would have been a luxury she didn't want."

She folded her hands on the tablecloth. "Is she the reason you're no longer a trainer?"

"She has a lot to do with it, yes."

"And you loved her?"

"Yeah," he admitted. "I did." Deeply. Painfully.

"Did she end it, or did you?"

"I suppose if I don't answer you, you'll continue to ask again and again."

"And again, Sir."

"Liz ended it." Except for Damien, no one knew how devastated he'd been. He and Damien had stayed up almost an entire night at the Den, drinking a bottle of the world's finest single malt. The next day, hating what he saw in the mirror, Alex had vowed never to look back.

"You haven't gotten involved with anyone since?"

"No. And I'm not planning to. D/s relationships can be more complex than ordinary ones. Be careful what you wish for."

She shuddered. "Warning heeded," she said.

"Ready?" He stood and offered his hand. "This time, you may follow me. Stay back about two feet."

She didn't answer, but she didn't protest. He knew his behaviour kept her off balance, and that was his intention.

He walked her to her car and waited while she programmed his downtown Golden address into her navigation system. He intended to drive so that she could follow, but he would expect her at his house again, and he never wanted to hear that she'd got lost.

It took less than fifteen minutes to arrive at his home. "I never expected you to live in a place like this," she said. "How old is it?"

"It's considered Victorian-style," he said. "Built after 1940. It was a foreclosure and needed a tremendous amount of work. One of Damien's friends did the restoration. It took about four months, but I think it was a good investment."

"It's charming," she said.

He didn't add that he'd bought it with the expectation he and Liz would live together. Then the Bartholomew deal went south and he hadn't got around to selling.

"The grounds are beautiful," she said while they stood together on the sidewalk.

"Landscaping company," he explained. "I wouldn't know a pansy from a petunia."

"You have both."

"Do I?"

"In those pots." She pointed.

He wondered if she was stalling.

"Shall we?" He headed up the three steps to the wraparound porch. As he unlocked the heavy wooden door, she wrapped her arms around her middle, despite the mild evening weather. "After you."

Inside, she gasped. "I hate to be rude, and I know this isn't protocol, but do you mind if I have a look around? This would be a perfect location for a charity fundraiser," she said.

"Do you ever stop?"

"Are you kidding me?" she countered. "This house was designed for entertaining."

When the remodel had been completed, he'd envisioned hosting parties for business associates, here, along with an occasional lifestyle function. That she saw what he did intrigued him. "You can place your purse there," he said.

"Would you like me to take off my shoes?"

"It's not necessary. Yet." But he appreciated her asking. He showed her the study, then the living room with its gas fireplace and stone hearth. He drew the curtains before heading towards the dining room, then the kitchen.

The largest chunk of his funds had been spent on this part of the house, ripping down walls, opening the space, adding a glassed-in breakfast nook. Since he didn't eat at home much, he took Marcus' word that the appliances were a chef's dream.

"I love the combination of classic and contemporary throughout the whole place," she said, running her fingers over the granite counters. "It really works. Seriously, Sir, you have to let me plan a party here."

Alex appreciated her enthusiasm. What he wouldn't have given for Liz to have fallen in love with the house like Chelsea seemed to. "There's a media centre downstairs," he said. "And the bedrooms are upstairs."

As if she were a guest rather than a sub who'd be screaming within half an hour, he gave her a tour of the upper story, including the master suite.

"You weren't kidding about the hook in the footboard of your bed," she said while rubbing her forearms.

"I don't joke about things like that. Now, go down to the living room. Strip. Leave your clothing and shoes near your purse. If the room is cold, there's a switch on the wall for the fireplace. I want you kneeling, facing the window."

She looked up at him. The air seemed to sizzle. "Yes, Sir," she whispered. Even the way she said it sounded submissive. Her tone as well as her volume had changed.

Without another word, she left. He went into the cupboard in the master closet and selected two instructional pieces, along with a tawse designed by Master Marcus Cavendish. Fancifully, Marcus had etched a dollar symbol into the leather, in honour of the first million-dollar deal Alex had brokered.

When he no longer heard sounds coming from downstairs, he joined her. He placed his belongings on a claw-footed end table, then rearranged a few things, waiting a long time before saying anything, testing her resolve. "Very nice," he said. She was kneeling up the way he'd instructed that night at the Den.

"Thank you, Sir."

"Louder."

She took a breath. "Thank you, Sir."

He folded his arms across his chest. "Inspect." He was pleased when she stood, her head up, looking straight ahead to the window. She placed her hands behind her head and thrust out her breasts. Finally she spread her legs. "You remembered."

"Yes, Sir."

She continued to look ahead even as he closed the distance. He walked around her a couple of times, and she remained perfectly in position. "And you shaved your cunt," he observed.

"I did, Sir."

"Mind if I see how good of a job you did?"

"Please go ahead, Sir."

He ran his hand over her bare mound, then slipped a finger between her folds. "Smooth," he said. "No stray hairs."

"You won't be needing the tweezers, Sir?"

"Not today." He dropped his hand. He knew she had expectations about how this procedure would work, so he changed it up. "Turn around and show me your ass."

She drew her eyebrows together for only a second to indicate her confusion, then she turned and bent to grab her ankles.

"Spread your cheeks."

She struggled a bit for balance as she complied.

"I want you to put a small plug up there every morning while you shower and get ready for work."

"Yes, Sir."

"Kneel up."

Her motions were slow and somewhat exaggerated. "You're struggling to do things, which tells me you haven't been practising. And that makes me question your commitment. I prefer to see your motions be flawless and elegant."

"I apologise, Sir."

"No need. I'll ensure you have plenty of time to practise, beginning now. Return to your former position, where you're showing me your ass, and then kneel up. Then go from kneel up to showing me your ass. We'll begin with twelve repetitions." He took a seat in a wingback arm chair and watched.

She'd turned on the fireplace, so a fine sheen of perspiration began to dot her back as she moved through the exercise.

"Stop thinking," he told her. "I shouldn't be able to hear you at all."

She went through another couple, and she seemed more natural.

"That's much better. Do you feel the difference?"

"Yes, Sir. I do."

By the end, her form began to suffer again. "When your training has finished, I expect you to be able to move with ease, from standing to kneeling, or from lying to kneeling. Any combination you can think of, such as from lying to showing your ass. Mix it up. Make sure you're comfortable in your body. That means I require you to practise when we are not together. I recommend several times per day."

"I understand, Sir."

He stood. "We discussed your posture several times."

Her green eyes were wide, and a bit of fear danced in them. "Am I going to be punished, Sir?"

"No. You will be instructed," he said. "We will reinforce the lesson as many times as necessary. I prefer to punish you for flagrant disregard of the rules. For example, now that you know you are required to practise moving between your positions, not doing so is reason for punishment." He picked up one of the items from the side table and showed it to her. "This is called a posture collar. It will keep your head and shoulders straight at all times. You will wear this tonight. Going forward, anytime you need correction, you'll fetch it for me. Stand with your hands behind your back. Feet shoulder-width apart."

She didn't blink as she stood in position.

"This is one of my favourites. It's strict, but not terribly uncomfortable." He showed her the wide collar. "This is padded, for your chin to rest on." He expected her to argue, but she remained silent. "Ready?"

"Yes, Sir."

He wrapped the stiff leather around her throat then moved behind her to secure its two metal buckles. He checked the fit before tightening more. "How is that?"

"Fine."

"Look down."

Instinctively she attempted to lower her chin. The collar restricted her movement.

"How is it, now?" he asked.

"Effective, Sir."

"There's a mirror over there. Go."

She reached up to touch the collar's three D-rings.

"I can attach a leash or secure your wrists, or tie you to any number of things."

"It's...it's a bit frightening, Sir."

"Please tell me your safe word." He was watching her reflection in the mirror, and he saw her wrinkle her nose.

"Parsley."

"Use that word to stop the scene at any time. If you're just a bit scared, you are welcome to ask to talk or use the word slow." He took her shoulders and turned her to face him. Damn, she had beauty that appealed to him on a primal level. He wanted her. Her eyes hid nothing, and he saw a mixture of desire and trust beneath the apprehension. For a moment, before he harnessed his thoughts, he thought about fucking her hard, and her grabbing hold of him as she surrendered. She was not his, he reminded himself ruthlessly. He'd screwed up once before. With Chelsea, he'd keep his emotional distance. "Return to the centre of the room and practise kneeling up from the inspect position. Do it ten times. You may use the rug."

"Thank you, Sir."

"You recalled your manners," he said. "Kneeling on the hardwood was uncomfortable, wasn't it?"

"Yes, Sir."

"So you understand that a rug is a luxury."

"I do."

"I'm glad you recognise that," he said. "Always remember to thank your Dom when he or she allows you a comfort."

"I will. Thank you, again, Sir."

He released her. As she slowly walked towards the rug, her hips swayed seductively. The wide collar had changed her normal gait. Keeping her in it permanently was a definite consideration.

On her bare feet, she crossed the room. He noticed she'd painted her toenails. If he remembered correctly, and it was possible he didn't, they'd been a coral colour at the Den. Tonight they were a fire-engine red. He was taken aback by how erotic it looked. His preference was for mile-high heels, but this woman was the sexiest thing he'd ever seen.

Forcing himself to focus, he picked up the rattan cane. She stumbled when she saw his approach. "I am not intending to use this for punishment," he assured her. "I prefer canes for instruction or for sensual play. I do not rule it out for correction, if necessary, but I would not surprise you with it."

"I appreciate that, Sir."

"But you can repeat that one. The idea is for you to be able to do what you need to, despite distractions. Focus." He stood close to her. He breathed in her scent, one that had haunted him since their night at the Den. Her body smelt slightly of vanilla, something light and fresh that could attract men from a ten-state region. But more intoxicating, it was layered with the heady scent of feminine arousal.

Once she had finished the sequence, he said, "Extend your hands." He attached fabric cuffs to her wrists then fastened those to the D-rings on her collar. "Another dozen."

"I won't be able to balance as well, and my legs are getting a bit cramped."

"In that case, we'll make it two dozen," he amended.

"I..."

He cocked one eyebrow.

She set her jaw and glared. "No."

He picked her up. She squirmed and squealed as he carried her to the chair. Since her arms were confined, manoeuvring her was more tricky than normal, but he managed to sit and get her body across his lap in a single, fluid move.

"Sir!"

"Generally I warm up a sub's skin before striking her. But this is meant as instant behaviour correction. I do not tolerate defiance. Think about this the next time you choose to be wilful." He reached for the tawse and used his legs to trap her lower body. He knew she was in an uncomfortable position, and being unable to brace her upper body had to be disconcerting. But he didn't allow any of those thoughts to dissuade him. "You'll receive eight spanks for your insolence, and you'll be grateful it isn't more."

She screamed as he laid the heavy forked leather strap across the backs of her thighs. He gave her no time to absorb the blow or reflect on it before laying it to her again and again.

When he was finished, her ass and the backs of her legs were coloured an angry red. "Any questions?" he asked.

"No."

"Anything else to add?"

"Thank you, Sir." Venom dripped from her voice.

He helped her to stand. "Now, naughty sub, you can perform your exercise or you can get dressed and go home. I have no energy for someone who intends to waste my time." Rather than let her go, he held her around the waist.

Tears swam in her eyes, but he refused to let her emotion soften him. He'd spanked her hard to teach her a lesson.

He released her long enough to stand himself, then he took her by the shoulders.

"I hated that," she said.

"Because?"

"It felt so impersonal, Sir."

"It was meant that way, Chelsea."

"And..."

"Go on."

"This collar, and the way my wrists are attached..."

"I'm listening."

"It just..." She looked up at him.

The moisture in her eyes made the green appear more startling. He waited. She frowned, then scowled. She blinked to erase the tears, and he saw her try to reach for her face, only to have the bondage restrict her movements. This woman bore little resemblance to the one who'd approached him so determinedly at the Den. She was softer, more vulnerable, but he also saw her internal confusion about what that meant to her.

"You were right. I wasn't prepared for it to be this difficult."

He nodded. "It takes a tremendous strength to subject yourself to someone else's will." At times, being a Dom, especially a trainer, wasn't easy, either. It could be an emotional minefield, and he sure as hell wasn't perfect and didn't always make the right choices. His failed relationship with Liz reinforced that. "You have a safe word and a way to slow things down. You never have to do anything you don't want to. And you can end things at any time," he reminded her.

She sighed.

"You've never looked more beautiful, with your red behind and your tears."

"I've never felt more humiliated, with my tears, and knowing I was punished for failing."

"You were not punished for failing," he said, digging his fingers into her reassuringly. He considered having her kneel or sit, but decided to allow her to stand while she sorted through the feelings from the spanking. "You were punished for your attitude."

"But if I had practised more —"

"Practised at all," he corrected.

She tried to nod, but the rigid leather around her throat wouldn't let her. He saw the frustration on her face. This, more than anything he could have possibly done, gave her a taste of what true submission was like. He saw her struggle and silently vowed to hold her until she admitted defeat or triumphed over her internal conflicts.

"If I had practised at all, I would be better at the whole kneeling thing."

"That part concerns me less than your defiance."

"I get that." She swallowed deeply. "At least I think I do. Until now, no one has ever seen me cry."

He believed that. "I'm honoured that you're not hiding that."

"I'm freaking trying to, Sir."

He smiled, appreciating her honesty. "So not being able to wipe your eyes is as difficult as the tears themselves, and maybe harder than being spanked?"

"I hadn't thought of it that way, but yes."

"I'd like you to release your conceptions. Crying means something different to you than it does to me." He moved one of his hands from her shoulder to her hair. He smoothed strands back from her forehead. "I frankly like it when my trainees cry. To me it signifies she's giving over some sort of control. It can mean she's hurt, chastised, or that she's enjoying the experience. I've found it can mean there's some sort of emotional change going on inside her. It's real and it's honest, and I appreciate it when it happens. Tears can be cathartic. You can embrace them or pretend to be brave." He flattened one palm against the back of her head. "But pretending to be brave will get in your way of embracing everything you're hoping to find."

"I'm feeling a little overwhelmed, Sir," she admitted.

"Understandable. I recommend we end the evening early."

"I thought we'd be together longer."

"That was my original plan. But I want you to take some time to think about what you want and what you're hoping to achieve through training. I want you to think about whether you're doing this for you or whether you're doing it simply to hook a man you think you like."

"I—"

"Hear me out." He held her tighter. "Doing this for anyone other than yourself will result in failure. That's not a judgement, that's a fact. Submission can be emotionally fraught. Make sure you're doing it for the right reasons."

"There's nothing wrong with trying it, is there, Sir? I didn't know I liked scallops until I had one at a party."

"We're not exactly talking apples to apples," he said with a grin.

"You're disappointed in me, Sir." She swallowed again.

He shook his head. "You will never disappoint me. There's a reason you chose your defiant behaviour. You should consider why that is. I expect you to need to work through things. Almost all subs do." Liz had been the exception. When she found something he hated, she did it over and over. "Before I release you from the collar and send you home, I'd like you to do the kneeling and standing exercise that I had instructed before your spanking. Of course, you're free to safe word and leave immediately." He could not and would not allow her tantrum to thwart his will.

"I'll finish," she whispered.

He released her.

She walked across the room, and he liked the sight of the fading red stripes left by his tawse.

He picked up his cane and went to stand near her. Because of the collar, she couldn't look away. No matter how badly she hated the thing, he decided he would continue to use it if she came back. And that was the big question. Would she return?

As she went through her motions, he gently used the cane to reposition her. "Remain standing," he said when she was finally finished. She was perspiring, and her breaths were a little laboured. "I'd like you to remain here," he said, "for less than sixty seconds. Can you do that?"

"Yes, Sir."

Some subs had a mental mindfuck if they were left alone, and he knew of some Doms who would use that as a punishment to exploit emotions. He wasn't a big fan of it, but he saw its purpose.

He went upstairs to the master bedroom to grab a tube of arnica. When he returned, he bent down behind her. "You only have a couple of minor welts on the backs of your thighs." He dabbed some cream onto each mark then used his fingertip to cover the reddened areas. "Take this home with you, and put on a bit more before bed. I doubt you'll bruise, however. You take the strap well." That would be good news for her, if she chose to continue her training.

"Thank you for doing that, and for the instruction, Sir."

"My pleasure," he told her as he stood. He'd forgotten how much he really enjoyed interacting with a sub.

He placed the tube of arnica next to her purse then returned to unclip her wrists. "You'll want to stretch, very gently, and maybe rotate your shoulders."

She did so, then he unbuckled the collar.

"Thank you, Sir." She placed her hands at her sides. "This feels a bit awkward."

"This?" he asked.

"Ending the evening prematurely. Me being naked. The way I am questioning everything I thought I wanted."

"I'll get you a bottle of water from the kitchen," he said, leaving her alone to dress...or not. He'd let her set their direction.

When he returned to the living room, she was perched on the arm of the couch, fully dressed, back in control.

He handed her the drink, and she uncapped it with a shaky hand.

She took a sip and looked up at him. "If we continue, will I have to wear that...thing again?"

"What is your objection to the posture collar?" He took a seat in his wing-backed chair.

"I don't like having my hands and motions restricted like that."

"Why?"

"Why?" she repeated.

"I find it to be an excellent training tool. If you thought about it objectively, you'd agree. So why do you hate having your motions restricted? Consider your answer. The first night, at the Den, you told me that you like to be tied up. Then when I attached you to the wall, you didn't do well with it."

She took another drink. "I think it's not necessarily about restricting my movements."

"Please. Go on."

"I guess I like to meet people as equals. When I can't move around freely, I don't feel equal. I'm also accustomed to communicating by nodding. I like to be able to lower my head. Does that make sense?"

"It does." He was glad she'd chosen to leave. She had a lot to think through. "If you elect to continue training, I will use the collar often for the reasons you outlined. It will reinforce your subservience along with my desire for you not to hide. I expect answers to my questions. Nodding allows you a way to avoid being verbal."

"What if I put it on my limits list?"

"You are free to do so. Is it uncomfortable? Too big? Too small?"

"No," she admitted, tilting her head and looking up at him through her lashes, a coyness the collar wouldn't permit.

"Think about it," he encouraged. "Will you have similar objections if I tie you to my bed? To a St Andrew's cross? Why did you enjoy the experience before playing with me?"

"Do I have to answer that?"

"Not right now. If you come back, I will certainly want to discuss it." He stood. "I'll walk you to your car."

She re-capped the bottle, then placed it on the side table. She picked up her purse and unclipped her keys from a small hook inside the biggest compartment.

"You're organised," he said.

"I don't like to misplace things." She placed the tube of ointment in an outside pocket.

It was then that he comprehended. "You like to be in control." Everything she did was precise, from the way she folded her clothes, to the way she'd placed her utensils at dinner, to the deliberate way she attached her keys and put everything in its place.

"Are you calling me a control freak?"

"Are you one?" he countered, not responding to her defensiveness.

"Some people might say that."

"Tell me again about your first experiences with BDSM, when you were tied up."

"I liked it." She paused. "It wasn't strict," she admitted. "I could get out of it."

"Did you?"

She shook her head then, apparently catching herself, said, "No. Knowing I could get out of it made it possible for me to tolerate it." She opened her eyes wide.

"The thing is, Chelsea, no matter how strict the bondage, you can always get out of it with your safe word. The difference is how you think about it."

"But I could get out of it just by moving my hands."

"Your way of thinking has more to do with it than anything else," he countered.

"But I was also being whipped."

"I spanked you," he pointed out. "The only difference," he said again, "is your thought process. I question your commitment. I encourage you to just enjoy an occasional scene, something to spice up your sex life. Give up the submission idea. You're not suited for it."

She set her chin at a mutinous angle.

"You just proved my point," he said. And in a way, that was a pity. He'd enjoyed his time with her, and he was sorry to see it end.

Chapter Five

Well, shit. She exhaled, gripping the car's steering wheel so tight that her knuckles whitened.

Chelsea had spent days trying to get Master Alexander's attention. When he hadn't called her after their night together at the Den, she'd telephoned Sara and asked Sara to put her in touch with some Doms, figuring that Master Alexander would hear about it. Chelsea had gambled that he would search her out.

She was accustomed to getting what she wanted. Her sights were set on landing him as a trainer. She *had* to have a trainer. Last weekend, she'd seen Master Evan C at another party. She'd approached him, and he'd asked if she knew more than she had the last time he saw her. When she'd shaken her head, he'd called her a poser. And he hadn't responded to a single solicitation she'd sent outlining how You're The Star could help him get ahead.

That was when she'd taken more drastic measures to ensure Master Alexander trained her.

When his name had shown up on her caller identification, she'd smiled.

Mission accomplished.

As usual.

But the evening they'd just spent together hadn't turned out the way she'd hoped.

It was as if he saw her deepest fears and exploited them, leaving her a confused wreck. Through her discussions with him and Gregorio at the Den, she knew there was more to this submissive thing than an occasional mind-blowing experience. She thought she'd understood the need to focus on her Dom's pleasures.

When she played with Master Alexander, though, everything became a jumble of emotional angst.

At home, she paced the confines of the apartment until she was afraid she'd wear a path in the hardwood floors. Sleep would be impossible until she'd sorted through the evening's events.

With a sigh, she changed into her swimsuit. Her apartment complex had some niceties, including indoor and outdoor pool facilities. She found water to be relaxing as well as restorative, and she did a lot of her best thinking in the bath as well as the building's hot tub. But as she was leaving her unit, she caught sight of the welts in the mirror.

She froze for a moment, remembering the way he'd effortlessly picked her up and deposited her across his lap for a brutal spanking.

It had been nothing like her previous, albeit limited, experiences.

The tawse had stung. It hadn't been fun or arousing. It had been punishment, pure and simple, a painful, awful expression of his displeasure. She'd hated it. She had felt as if she would drown in her humiliation, and she'd been pissed off that he was treating her that way, like she was an errant pupil. Gregorio had told her that subs were corrected all the time. In theory, that was fine. But enduring it was another thing entirely.

She grabbed a long terrycloth robe from the closet and fiercely knotted the belt at her waist. With any luck, no one else would be using the hot tub.

Other than a couple of teenage boys who were horsing around in the deep end of the pool, she had the area to herself.

She turned on the jets to drown out their noise, then removed the robe and sank in deep, letting the water bubble around her chest. Eventually, she closed her eyes and leaned her head back.

Yeah, she was pissed off. And if she were honest, she'd admit she was as angry with herself as she was with Master Alexander.

He'd given her everything she said she wanted. And damn him, he made her question the course she'd set for herself. She hated that he was right, that she had some serious thinking to do.

Why couldn't things be simpler?

She replayed their evening. Once she'd got past the discomfort of having him place her dinner order, she had enjoyed the experience of being cared for. Her entire life, she and her mother had fought and struggled for their place in the world. She'd never relaxed and drank her wine while someone else handled the details. And he'd done a good job, soliciting opinions and ensuring her needs were met.

It had been better than she'd expected, and she'd had to remind herself she was being trained, rather than on a date.

At his house, the message had been clear. She wasn't his submissive. She was simply someone who had hired him to do a job.

He'd treated her as if she were chattel, rather than a respected equal.

She opened her eyes.

When she'd set her course, she'd had the idea that it would be a lot of fun. They would have two weeks together that would include some sex, a whole lot of arousal, a few orgasms, being tied up, and some beatings. They'd try some wild and wonderful things that she'd only read about and, hopefully, some she'd never even heard of.

She hadn't anticipated that it would include things she found humiliating. What was worst about that was that she hadn't known ahead of time that she'd find anything upsetting. That first night, they'd talked about limits. She'd been honest that she didn't think she had any. But that was before physical acts caused unexpected responses.

If she were honest with herself, she would also admit she hadn't expected it to be so much work. Holding up her arms, kneeling, being spanked and restrained taxed her body.

This whole thing was frustrating. She kept intellectualising the process of submission. But it turned out the more she thought she knew, the more she realised she still had to learn. It was as if once she understood something, there was another layer to be explored.

Several more teens came down to the pool area, and so she went back upstairs. As she showered, she remembered him asking if she was a control freak. She shampooed her hair and considered the question. She supposed the description fit.

She took down the handheld showerhead and rinsed off. Being a control freak probably didn't make a good sub.

She'd read about subs who were naturals and others who embraced it after learning about it. She was definitely in the latter category, if she could get there at all.

Despite her hesitations, even after her problems this evening, she was drawn to certain things. And she'd liked it a whole lot more at the Den when he'd fucked her and brought her to orgasm. There was an intimacy about the way they interacted that she'd found lacking in her previous relationships.

In retrospect, the kneeling, being in the posture collar, having her hands secured, even the spanking wasn't all bad. He'd never hurt her, and even at his roughest, he'd ensured her safety, and he'd talked to her the entire time.

He had been right when he said that everything she experienced was coloured by her perceptions. The thick leather collar was only bad if she allowed it to be. It hadn't been all that uncomfortable to wear. He'd made sure it wasn't too tight, and the inside was lined so it didn't chafe her skin. She'd been able to rest her chin on the top.

She wondered how different their scene might have been if she had stopped the internal struggle. At most, she would have been confined in it for a couple of hours, and if luck held, she might have ended up with an earth-shattering orgasm.

She moved the showerhead down her body, from her chest to her belly, then between her legs. She used one hand to part her pussy folds. Tonight's interaction had left her with raw feelings. She hadn't become very aroused. There were times—like when he entered the living room and she was naked near the fireplace, that she was aware of him, his proximity, his masculine power—that she'd started to be a little turned on. But then he'd kept himself remote.

The realisation stunned her.

She'd been hoping for something different. Even that night at the Den, she'd hated it when he seemed impersonal with her, and she had told him so. But at the end of the evening he'd fucked her. The connection had soothed her and made everything else okay.

At his house, that had been missing.

She didn't want him to interact with her as if she were just any random woman. She'd seen the way he treated Brandy. And Chelsea wanted something more meaningful. Heaven help her, she'd wanted sex, hugs, even caresses.

Some of her previous boyfriends would be shocked by that admission. She'd always hated to snuggle. One man had called her cold, another had said she was standoffish.

So now what?

She wanted Master Evan C. Master Alexander wasn't interested in her.

In order to be successful at training, she knew she would have to keep the relationship with Master Alexander professional, as if he were any other teacher. That he saw her nude and could do almost anything with her body was beside the point.

She continued to move the showerhead between her legs. She turned the dial so that the water pulsed, rather than sprayed, and she teased her clit with the warmth and the pressure.

The orgasm she'd wanted loomed out of reach. She rose onto the balls of her feet and clenched her buttocks, striving for completion.

She needed pressure on her nipples, she realised. And with the way she was using the showerhead, there was no way to do that.

A minute or so later, she gave up in frustration. Until he'd introduced her to the more extreme BDSM, she'd been able to get off easily. Now she wanted exquisite sensations everywhere.

The water ran cold, and she turned off the faucet.

After drying off, she took the tube of arnica from her purse and crossed the bedroom to stand in front of the cheval mirror.

The welts were almost all gone. But there was one that still looked a bit raw. She squirted ointment onto her fingertip and then dabbed it on the red mark.

Her breath caught as she recalled the way he'd picked her up and deposited her across his lap. He'd been perfunctory in his punishment, but it hadn't been brutal. He hadn't expected an apology, rather, he'd encouraged her to consider what caused her to react the way she had.

She recapped the tube and froze, recalling the way he'd treated her at the Den. No one had ever tormented her breasts the way he had, and she had liked having them distended. The exquisite line between pain and pleasure had made her orgasms so powerful.

Chelsea told herself she should go to bed. Instead, she put on a pair of yoga pants and a T-shirt and buried herself in housework, trying to ignore the truth that was nagging at her—she wanted to continue her training.

But she couldn't fault him for being frustrated, even if he insisted she'd never disappointed him. He had done his part, and she'd shown up without practising anything that would make her a good sub.

She recalled the way Brandy had knelt at the Den, and the way she'd executed his commands. The woman hadn't questioned anything, and she hadn't blushed with embarrassment when he'd issued orders. Instead, she'd moved from position to position with confidence. And Chelsea knew that mastery came from practice.

Why had she thought submission to be anything different from anything else she'd ever learnt?

She might decide he was right, that it wasn't for her, and that she should be satisfied with an occasional scene. There had been moments during her times with Master Alexander when she'd felt at peace, when she'd harnessed her mind and stayed in the moment, which was a real change from the way she spent the rest of her life.

Since it was late, probably too late to call him, she decided to do the one thing she knew would please him and test her commitment. Despite the fact she was tired and more than a little sexually frustrated, she set an alarm on her phone for twenty minutes.

She knelt, then practised moving between the positions he'd taught her, from kneeling up to standing, from kneeling back to inspect. After a few minutes, the repetition became uncomfortable. Her muscles started to fatigue, and she glanced at the timer. *Damn.* She was only halfway through.

Drawing on the same determination that had got her this far in life, she kept going.

With five minutes to go, she realised how badly her body hurt, and she was thinking of all the other things she could do be doing, like a load of laundry, paying some bills, making a grocery list, even getting some much-needed sleep. Not that insomnia wouldn't keep her awake, regardless.

But instead of giving in and quitting, she harnessed her runaway thoughts. She pictured him, his legs spread in a commanding way. Then she imagined him ordering her onto her back so he could lick her cunt.

She stumbled.

The man had the power to discombobulate her, even when he wasn't there. She should have conjured that image while she had been in the shower. The orgasm would have been there for sure.

By the time the alarm rang, she was sweating. She had to give credit to Brandy. The woman had made things look easy As Chelsea had just learnt, it took a lot of work to make elegance appear effortless.

The next morning, she got up a little early so she could practise before going to the office. And at her lunch break, she gathered up all her courage and telephoned Master Alexander.

He answered on the first ring.

"You were right," she said before he could say anything beyond hello.

"About what, in specific?"

His voice, so rough, so sexy, made her toes curl in her pumps. "I was being a control freak, questioning everything." She left out the bit that he'd been too impersonal with her. Admitting that would be far too difficult. And clouding their arrangement with emotional need wouldn't be good for either of them. "I know it's a lot to ask, but I want to continue my training, if you'll have me."

"I don't give a lot of second chances." His tone was flat and less than encouraging.

She continued on, regardless. "I don't blame you." She paced back and forth in front of her office window. "But I'm asking." She took a breath and stood still. "Please."

"What changed your mind?"

She should have realised this wouldn't be easy, that he'd ask dozens of questions. "I did a lot of thinking last night. I do want to get Master Evan C's attention. But I want to experience this for my sake, as well. There's something appealing about giving up control. I can't believe I'm saying this, but I found it somewhat relaxing, after I got past my thoughts and accepted the experience."

He remained silent for so long she thought he might not answer. When he did, she felt as if he'd sucked all the enthusiasm from her veins. "I expect you to practice your positions every day for half an hour. Some days you should wear lingerie and heels. Other times, you should be naked. I also expect you to get checked out by a physician and be prepared to show me the test results. If you can manage all that without complaint for a week, and *if* you're still interested, contact me again."

Without another word, he ended the call.

In shock, she stared at the blank screen.

Traffic passed by and she barely noticed it. She'd been prepared for him to say no or to accept her back with a punishment. But she hadn't been prepared for a conditional yes.

She hated being tested. She'd made her decision. Why the hell couldn't he forgive her?

Frustration bubbling inside her, she resumed pacing. Then, realising that wasn't helping to dispel the agitation gnawing at her, she dropped her phone on her desk. She took her seat and drew several steadying breaths. The maddening, irritating man always gave her plenty of opportunity to work on schooling her thoughts, which, she supposed, was part of being a good sub. And that was exactly his point.

She'd heard in his tone that he expected her to fail.

And that was not an option.

Every day for the next week, she did as he'd instructed. After getting out of bed, she went through the motions for fifteen minutes. She did the same for a quarter of an hour after work, no matter how late she got in or how exhausted she was. And because every part of her ached, she soaked in the hot tub every day.

The first couple of days, she'd had difficulty reining in her thoughts. Then it had become somewhat easier. By the last part of the week, she'd been able to go through the paces with a certain amount of grace and a whole lot less of a brain fuck.

This time when she called him, she got his voicemail. She sighed with frustration as she listened to his greeting, but she put a smile on her face—a technique she'd learnt at a sales training event—and left a pleasant message.

All day, she jumped every time her phone rang. And she even checked the screen several times, even though she knew for a fact it had been silent. That night, when she was in bed, he finally telephoned. She exhaled a few times to steady herself before answering. "Good evening, Sir." It amazed her how the words themselves made her feel calmer.

"You're certain you want to continue forward?"

"I am, Sir."

"Tell me why."

"I want to learn. In fact, I already am learning to quiet my thoughts. It's surprising to me, but I'm more focused at work, and I am feeling more creative."

"You realise I will be able to tell right away if you're telling the truth about any of this."

She gritted her teeth. "Of course, Sir."

"And this is your last chance. I will not accept you back again after this."

Her heart leapt into her throat. "This means you are accepting me back?"

"For two weeks," he said. "And only if I see significant improvement in your attitude and proof that you've done what you said you have."

She refused to challenge him, another first for her. Instead, she said, "Thank you." She ignored the fact her hand was shaking. Until he'd agreed, she hadn't realised just how important his answer was. "Thank you, Sir."

"Do you remember where I live?"

"It's still programmed into my navigation system, Sir."

"Are you available to start tomorrow evening?"

"I am, Sir."

"Very well. Six o'clock?"

She tossed back the blankets and climbed from bed. "Is there anything specific I should wear?"

"You'll be naked the moment the door closes behind you, so it doesn't matter."

When she didn't respond right away, he asked, "Question?"

"I presume you'll open the door and then I'll strip?" She started to pace, a habit she'd picked up since she'd started seeing him.

"Let yourself in, remove your clothing, and wait by the fireplace."

"Yes, Sir."

"Have you been masturbating?"

Heat chased through her body. "Not successfully," she said. "I mean, I tried." She stumbled through the admission while he remained silent. "I did, masturbate that is, with the showerhead."

"And you didn't climax?"

"No, Sir."

"Good. From here forward, you will come only when I give permission."

"I…" She trailed off and inhaled before saying, "Yes, Sir."

"Being good doesn't come easy to you, does it, Chelsea?"

"May I have permission to come tonight, Sir?"

"Absolutely not."

Since he'd denied it, need crawled through her. Right now, she knew even the gentlest of touches against her clit would get her off. She could feel her pulse there, demanding. Confound him.

"Don't be late, Chelsea."

He said the last word with a soft inflection that made her heart stop. That had sounded personal, and her body reacted. "I will be there, Sir."

In bed, she couldn't get comfortable, and she was certain he had planned it that way. She was aware of the ache in her pussy that a simple touch would vanquish. Her breasts felt full, and she desperately wanted to play with her nipples.

She thumped her pillow into a different shape, and that didn't help, either.

Finally, half an hour later, in abject frustration, she climbed out of bed and went through her paces again, while wearing her pyjamas. If she took off her clothes, she would be tempted to touch herself.

The act of thinking of her Dom rather than herself helped calm her.

As always, sleep eluded her. She thought wryly about the posture collar. Having her hands secured seemed like the best way to resist temptation. So she would just have to use willpower.

She turned on her side and shoved both hands beneath her head. She forced herself not to think about her upcoming time with Master Alexander, and instead, she counted sheep, something she hadn't done since she was a child.

It must have worked because the alarm dragged her to a groggy consciousness. She hit the snooze button often enough that she was running late for an appointment with a potential new client. The coffeemaker took too long and she glared at it, as if that would hurry it along.

She was pouring the first cup when she remembered she still needed to practise her movements.

With a frustrated sigh, she looked at the clock on the microwave. Since she'd done extra the day before, surely that put her ahead for today. She dragged a hand through her hair, wishing it worked that way. Either she intended to keep her word, or not. If she'd got up when the alarm rang, she wouldn't be in a time crunch.

She took a long drink of the much-needed caffeine then, in the middle of the kitchen, she knelt. It took a lot of mental effort to keep herself calm rather than panicking about the time. But after half an hour, she leapt up and headed for the bathroom.

Fortunately her potential new client called to say he was running late, and she arrived at her office two minutes ahead of him.

She presented her proposal, and he signed on the dotted line. And of course, she and her team would have to begin work immediately to promote his upcoming independent movie. Still, that didn't stop her and Jennifer, her administrative assistant, from grabbing hold of each other and screaming before doing a dance around the office. Finally! Years of work, scraping and scrimping, paying off bills and the business was getting the success she thought it deserved.

The rest of the day passed in a blur, and they even had lunch brought in.

Too soon, four-thirty arrived. Even though they'd been swamped, thoughts of being with Master Alexander had intruded. She'd been relieved to stay busy all day, otherwise she wasn't sure how she'd have survived the nine hours.

She hurried home for a shower, and to shave properly before meeting him. The sensual tension that had been simmering through her body heated to a boil. And she realised she was horny.

The battle with the clock that had begun around dawn continued, and she hurried out to the car. Of course, rush-hour traffic slowed her down. Fear that she was going to be late made her grip the steering wheel and scowl at one driver who was driving too slowly. She turned up the radio to distract her only to turn it back down when it added to her irritation. She arrived at his home in Golden one minute ahead of time.

Chelsea allowed her shoulders to collapse against the seatback then released the clawlike grip she'd had on the steering wheel. She fluffed her hair with her fingers before climbing out of the car and heading up the path to the front door. This time her nerves were stretched so taut she barely noticed the gorgeous landscaping or the foothills behind the Victorian-style house.

She smoothed her skirt, straightened her shoulders and knocked. He didn't answer. Feeling a little uncertain, she tested the knob. Since it was unlocked, she let herself in. She called out a greeting, but she got no response.

Remembering his directions, she moved into the living room and took off her clothes and shoes, leaving everything in an organised pile.

Near the fireplace, she lowered herself to the kneel up position and waited.

She couldn't help but notice a number of items on the side table. Her blood chilled at the sight of a cane, the dreaded collar, a box of surgical gloves, lube, several coiled lengths of restraints, and a curved metal hook. She couldn't tell for certain if that was the tawse or something else that lay across the arm of the couch.

Rather than looking at the intimidating assortment of paraphernalia, she forced herself to stare at the lamp. She jumped at every odd noise, as she wasn't sure whether Master Alexander was in the house or not. He hadn't called to change their plans. And she'd done what he told her to. She was starting to feel a bit uncomfortable, debating if she should stay there or go looking for him when she heard the sound of his footfalls on the hardwood floor.

Her chest rose and fell, and it was almost impossible to remain as she was while she waited for him. And he didn't say anything for a long time. Each moment felt interminable. Even if she hadn't heard his approach, she would have recognised his scent of crisp mountain pine. He smelt of the outdoors, and she responded on a visceral level. This man, this Dom, confused her in ways no one else ever had.

Her pulse slammed into overdrive. She was glad she'd called him and grateful he'd agreed to see her.

"Very good," he said. "Please present yourself for inspection."

The sound of his voice scrambled what was left of her thoughts. Thank God she had spent so much time practising. Her motions were almost automatic and much more refined than the last time he'd seen her.

She stood. Mindful of her posture, she kept her head up and looked straight ahead. She drew her shoulder blades together, then parted her legs and waited.

"You have been working on that," he said.

"Yes, Sir. I want to please you."

He didn't acknowledge that she'd spoken. "Open your mouth."

Fear gripped her that he'd put the dam in her mouth again, but he didn't.

Surprising her, he said, "Close it."

He never did what she expected.

"You've shaved again."

"Yes, Sir." She wasn't sure whether he'd expected an answer or not.

Even though he stepped back and a bit to the side, she continued to look ahead. Since she didn't want the thick collar fastened around her neck, and further, she wanted to prove her commitment, she was determined to do what he demanded of her.

"Present your breasts."

Though he hadn't asked that of her before, she'd seen Brandy do it at the Den. Chelsea lifted her breasts and drew them together, hoping she was doing it right.

"Perfect. Pinch your nipples."

She did it harder than she liked, because she knew he expected it. He stood there, watching as she applied the pressure. She continued to do as she was told, without question, even though it was becoming more and more painful.

"Now release them and part your pussy lips."

He was being cold with her, and she fought against her instinctive rebellion. She should have expected this. She made her movements as elegant as possible.

His inspection of her inner lips as he felt for stray hairs wasn't as brutal as the demonstration he'd given her at Master Damien's, but she could have been a stranger to him for all the attention he paid her. This was perfunctory. Or at least it would be unless he found she'd been remiss. And she'd for damn sure not been remiss.

"Show me your ass."

She swallowed deeply and lowered herself to all fours, facing the fire. She placed her forehead on the floor, then reached back with both hands to part her ass cheeks.

Like he had earlier, he regarded her. Or at least that was what she thought he was doing. He made no sound to indicate any movement.

Even though her heart was thumping, she stayed where she was, open and exposed. No doubt this was a test. She vowed not to fail this time.

After a while, she heard him moving around the room. She resisted the temptation to turn her head and peek.

She felt something press against her anus.

"Open up, naughty sub."

She closed her eyes and bore down. He inserted something, probably his finger, and probed her, stretching her hole.

"Have you ever worn a plug?"

"No, Sir."

"And what you mean is, no sir, not until now."

"No, Sir," she repeated. "I have not worn a plug until now."

He didn't tell her what he was doing, and she felt him insert a second finger. She moved just a bit to accommodate him.

"Now I'm going to put a small plug in your ass. It's a starter one, and you could perhaps tolerate something bigger. But I'll expect you to work up to something much, much larger over the next few days."

She'd never experimented much anally, and she wasn't sure how much she wanted to now. But she understood some Doms would want or expect it. For a moment, she thought of Master Alexander fucking her hard up the ass while she screamed in pleasure. Then, remembering her ultimate goal, she replaced the image with one of Master Evan C.

"Please turn your head and look at this."

He crouched next to her. Their faces were mere inches apart, and the intimacy startled her. She'd forgotten how devastatingly good-looking he was. He wore black trousers and a white dress shirt, with the sleeves turned up to his elbows. Judging by the stubble on his jaw, he'd obviously missed his morning shave. That made him appear all the more dangerous.

His deep, rich brown eyes arrested her attention. She might have believed he was being impersonal with her, but his expression said otherwise. A small frown burrowed between his eyebrows, and his gaze was focused on her. For an instant, the connection sizzled with electricity. She blinked first.

"This is the butt plug that is going up your ass on the first try without you carrying on. Are you clear?"

Though the widest part didn't appear much bigger around than the two fingers he'd just inserted inside her, the plug was long, and it had a base that would hold it in place.

"Do you remember your safe word?"

"Yes, Sir." She stared at the piece of moulded silicone. "Parsley, Sir."

"Ask me to put it in place."

She'd convinced herself that he wasn't as beastly as she sometimes remembered, but five minutes together had proved that wasn't true. "Please, Sir, will you put that...nasty thing in me?"

He smiled. "Lucky for you I'm not marking you down for lack of enthusiasm."

"Sorry, Sir," she said, looking at him and trying not to smile herself. "Shall I try again?"

"Do."

"Please, I beg you, Sir. I want you to put that hot thing straight up my ass."

This time he laughed, but he also he smacked her left butt cheek, hard. "If you insist," he responded.

He left her for a moment. She heard the unmistakable sound of lube being squirted onto the length of the plug. His polished wingtips sounded both loud and powerful on the floor as he returned.

"Spread your cheeks farther," he said.

Her Dom placed the unyielding tip against her opening. The thing had appeared flexible, so she hadn't been prepared for its unwelcome feel.

"Bear down...*now.*"

He pushed ahead, and she tried to allow it in.

Chelsea had to fight his momentum and her desire to escape in order to stay in position. Through gritted teeth, she told him, "This is way more difficult than a finger, Sir. Damn it!"

"Almost there. You can do it."

She whimpered. He continued to push.

She swore softly as the widest part pressed against her sphincter. Then she heard a sound like a pop, the plug slid all the way in and she sighed with relief when the pain subsided.

"Very pretty."

Although she didn't argue, she doubted the red thing looked attractive at all.

He twisted it so that the hilt was seated between her buttocks.

She gave an unladylike grunt. "Not a fan of that," she said. "Sir."

"Too bad. Now kneel back. I want to speak with you."

Wildly she wondered if she'd already upset him. But damn, that had hurt more than she'd expected. Frustrated with herself for expressing displeasure, she moved into position and kept her gaze straight ahead.

"You may relax and look at me." He removed his gloves and tossed them in the trash, then he sat on the sofa. "Do you still want to continue?"

She adjusted herself, trying to find a comfortable position with the plug inside her. The slick silicone felt different from his finger. It made her feel full. She was dealing with the intrusion because it pleased her Dom. She couldn't move without being aware of it inside her.

"Chelsea?"

"I'm just trying to think about how to deal with this butt plug, Sir."

"Quit thinking and allow it to be."

That was easy for him to say. He didn't have a long thing stuck up his rear channel. Because she was so aware of it, it dominated her thoughts.

"Lie on your back," he instructed. "You may use the rug."

She knew better than to argue.

The thing moved about as she awkwardly did as he said. Her movements were exaggerated as she tried not to move too much.

"Now, draw your knees to your chest and keep them there."

She closed her eyes, imagining the sight she made, with her pussy and the base of the plug revealed to him. She'd never been shy, even in bed, but this was an entirely new level of exposure. He expected a tremendous amount from her. And she hadn't been here half an hour.

"Stop the struggle."

Chelsea thought he might sit, but he remained standing, close to her. It didn't take long for the position to become uncomfortable. Air whispered from the nearby vent and cooled her hot pussy. She tried to harness her thoughts and relax into the moment.

When she shifted a bit, he moved to the table and returned. He showed her the cane.

"Again, I will never hit you with this without you being prepared, but I will use it to correct you."

She closed her eyes. At home, alone, it was easy to rationalise submission, and she could convince herself it wasn't all that bad and that he never demanded more than she could give. But it became a different thing when she was in the middle of it.

No matter what he said, she didn't want that rattan on her body, so she remained still.

"Good."

She held onto his approval. A simple word from him provided huge encouragement.

He left her there for so long that she stopped thinking about the plug and only about him. Her breathing evened out. She would have said it was impossible to tolerate the plug, but she would have been wrong.

"How is that?"

"Fine, Sir."

"Would you like to continue your training?" he asked eventually.

"Yes. Yes, please, Sir."

"In that case, I'm going to fuck your ass with that plug, and you're going to encourage me to go faster and harder."

She wrapped her hands tighter around her legs.

"Aren't you, Chelsea?"

Her breath was shaky.

"It seems you need time to work through various aspects of submission, that you naturally want to rebel."

"I hate for that to be true, Sir."

He stood close, tapping the cane against his ankle. He loomed over her, large, broad and imposing. Being in this position, looking up at him reinforced their roles.

"Am I wrong?" he asked.

"No." She wanted to drag her hand through her hair or fold her arms across her chest, but he compelled her to remain open. "Are you sure you have the patience for this? For me?"

"Yeah. I do. I consider it all to be part of your training," he said.

For the first time, she understood that this couldn't be easy for him, either. Why would he choose to tolerate a recalcitrant and stubborn woman when he could have his pick of already-perfect submissives?

In so many ways, he was an enigma. She'd learnt a little about him through online searches, but she only knew those things that put him in the press. It appeared he didn't participate in any social networking, and even though they'd been together a couple of times, it occurred to her that she didn't know much about him.

"You're doing fine," he assured her. "We'll work together until you give up the struggle. I appreciate that you're trying, that you're thinking. I've told you before, you will never disappoint me."

"But you tanned my hide last time, Sir."

"You will be punished swiftly and harshly for a bad attitude and for not following rules," he clarified. "But that doesn't mean I'm displeased with you, just an aspect of your behaviour. Again, I'm going to fuck your ass. We can use the plug you already have, or we can use a larger one?"

"No. No, Sir. This one is fine."

"On all fours, if you please."

When she didn't move fast enough, he tapped her with the cane to encourage her.

"Your choice, you can remain as you are or you can put your head on the floor and reach back to hold your buttocks apart."

That wasn't an easy decision. If she stayed as she was, it might be more difficult for him to get the plug in and out. On the other hand, if she moved, it would be easier to lose her balance. In the end, she asked, "Is it acceptable for me to..." Some of their conversations mortified her. "Stick out my bottom a bit?"

"Your decision," he said. "Doms may not always offer you that choice. Be aware."

"Yes, Sir." She pushed out her rear in his direction, waiting with huge impatience.

"It's customary to thank a Dom when he grants you a favour."

"Sorry, Sir," she apologised straightway. "And thank you for your generosity."

"I'll reinforce the lesson later."

Her whole body went rigid. She'd already earned a punishment? Would she ever learn? Posture. Manners. Tone of voice. A million things went into making a good submissive and she despaired of ever remembering them all at the same time.

She felt him grasp the plug.

"The more you relax, the easier this will be."

He pulled out the plug. She barely had time to absorb the shock of being stretched then having it out before he shoved it in again.

He pounded her relentlessly, and she was gasping and shaking, moving forwards and back as he fucked her with it. The dull throb of anguish overwhelmed her, leaving her unable to think.

"How is it?" he asked.

"It's..." Horrible. Awful. Hideous. And unbelievably, as he continued, as she moved with him instead of fighting to remain still, she started to become aroused. She'd never imagined it was possible to get turned on from anal penetration, but she was. "Sir!"

"Yes?"

"I... Oh, my God, I think I might come."

All of a sudden, with the plug out, he stopped.

She swore beneath her breath.

Silence shrouded the living room, and the temperature seemed to drop.

"Thank you for telling me," he said.

Unreleased need vibrated through her. She had no idea how long it had been since she'd had an orgasm. Days? Weeks? "Sir?"

"I have no objection, in general, to letting you orgasm, but this was not the appropriate time. I'd prefer to keep you on the edge for a while longer."

She gritted her teeth to keep her mouth shut. This submission thing became more and more difficult instead of easier.

"Since your ass is stretched and so wide open, I'm going to put in a larger plug."

Instinctively she tightened her buttocks.

"It's going in," he said. "How difficult do you want it to be?"

She heard him moving around the room, and not knowing what he was doing made her crazy.

"Would you like to see it?"

"No." She barely remembered to express her gratitude. "No, thank you, Sir." Knowing what was coming might make it worse.

"I'm doing this because you didn't remember to thank me earlier."

More than anything, she wanted to look at him, see his eyes, maybe gather some reassurance from the way he looked at her. "I thought you were going to spank me for that?"

"There are many ways to reinforce lessons," he said. "Corporal punishment is only one of several."

"I think I prefer that, Sir, to something else you might choose."

"As your Dom, I will make that decision."

This relationship was a juxtaposition. The things she liked most about him, that he was firm and unyielding, were also the things she hated the most.

"You were going to have to work your way up to a larger plug, regardless. This just accelerates my timeline."

"Yes, Sir," she said, feeling miserable. When would she learn to keep her mouth shut?

"Look at me, Chelsea."

She turned her head. Thankfully he had the plug behind his back.

"You are here for training. Of course you'll make mistakes, plenty of them. That's to be expected. We only have two weeks together. We have to move forward every day in order to accomplish what you want. I don't hold grudges. I don't expect perfection."

His reassurance was all she needed to settle back down. "I understand, Sir. I'm ready."

"Good girl."

He moved, and she thrust out her rear again. She made a decision not to feel embarrassed. He was going to do this whether she protested or not. She could stall or use a safe word, but eventually his will would prevail. So why not get on with it?

Although she hadn't heard him squirt lube on the plug, it was slick against her anus. He pressed it against her. This one felt big, beastly. She whimpered. She should never have complained about the smaller one.

He had only managed to insert it part of the way when he pulled it back out. "You can do this, Chelsea."

"Do what, Sir? Be torn asunder?"

"Bear down," he advised. He forced the thing in deeper.

"I... Fuck this!"

"Stop fighting me," he said.

"I'm trying to cooperate, Sir."

"In that case, relax your sphincter."

She wondered how many more times he could say the same thing with different words? And when would she finally listen?

He worked the thing in, then eased it out, going a little deeper and farther each time. It was so much thicker than the other one. "I'm not sure I can manage this, Sir!"

"You can," he said, his tone both encouraging and soothing.

She was afraid his determination was no match for her inability to take the plug's girth. Feeling helpless, desperate for this to be over, she inched away from him, trying to escape.

"Stick out your ass, Chelsea." He reached forward and took hold of her left shoulder to hold her in place.

She screamed when he stretched her ass even farther.

"That's it," he said. "It's going in. *Now.*"

With his hand on her shoulder, he forced her backwards, and he shoved the plug deep.

Tears swam in her eyes. She hated this. Hated him.

"You're there," he said.

Like she had with the previous one, she felt her anus relax around the stem of the plug after it was completely seated.

"That looks hot, Chelsea."

His approval made everything worthwhile.

"I really am looking forward to fucking you up the ass. Maybe even tomorrow."

She gulped for air, trying to steady her trembling body. He stroked his fingertips up and down her spine. She appreciated the luxurious calm that enveloped her.

"How does the plug feel?" he asked.

She hated to admit it, but now that it was in, it wasn't too bad. In fact, the full sensation, compounded by the fact he liked the way it looked, made her feel slightly sexy. How was that possible?

"Chelsea?"

"It's fine, Sir."

He squatted next to her and captured her face between his palms. "Did you want to thank me for putting it in you?"

Maybe in another lifetime. She blinked back the tears that stung her eyes. "Thank you, Sir. I appreciate your patience." When had she become such an adept liar?

He smiled, as if he'd read her mind and knew she hadn't been telling the truth. But that didn't seem to matter as much to him as the fact she'd followed protocol. "In future, Chelsea, I expect not to have to remind you. Please express your gratitude on a continual basis. For my attention, for teaching you, for punishing you, for my patience, everything."

"Yes, Sir," she whispered, entranced by the deep, rich depths of his eyes. She had never felt closer to him. "I know I am difficult, and I do appreciate you, more than you know. Thank you."

"Was the carrying on worth it?"

"No, Sir. But it freaking hurt!"

"Did that change anything?"

"You know it didn't, Sir."

"Next time, when it's either a bigger plug or my cock, push back and open yourself. It may not be easy, but it will certainly be more pleasant. But know this, Chelsea, your tears and protests will never sway me."

"Yes, Sir. Thank you for that." Her heart felt as if it might melt. In such a short time, this man had come to matter to her.

He moved one hand from her face and smoothed her hair.

It was as if no one knew her like he did. Because he demanded honesty, refused to allow games, didn't let her get away with prevarication, held her accountable, pushed her through her feminine embarrassment, he'd seen aspects of her personality even she hadn't known existed. There was a bratty part. She wasn't proud of that. He'd also discovered fears she didn't realise she had. For the first time with a man, she'd felt emotionally needy, and when she did, she didn't have to ask him to hold her. Somehow he knew to do it.

"The Dom who ends up with you will be one lucky man."

For a moment, she wished that man were him.

Chapter Six

"You may kneel back."

That quickly, he re-established his authority.

He released her, and she shook her head to clear it. She'd be a fool to fall for him. He was her trainer. Nothing more. She concentrated deeply so she would please him.

"Nice," he said.

It amazed her how much she loved hearing his approval. He stood near her, tall, masculine and for the moment, her entire world.

"Shall we discuss your training schedule? We have only a short time together, and a number of things to cover. Of course we will spend a considerable amount of time on anal."

She wrinkled her nose, attempting to stay on even footing and not succumb to the emotion that was coming with every step she ventured deeper into submission. "I was afraid of that, Sir."

"As well as holding your tongue." He smiled.

She grimaced.

"We'll also work on being bound and restrained, service and how to take a beating. We've had some time apart. Is there anything you'd like to add to your limits list?"

"No, there isn't."

"Your Dom will expect you to be excellent at giving head, so you'll spend time practising that, as well."

"I have my test results in my purse, Sir."

"I'll give you mine, as well."

"Can I ask a question about that?"

"Of course."

"We had sex at the Den..."

"Would you prefer we didn't fuck?"

"No." She chose her words. "I know you don't want things to be confused, but I would like you to fuck me."

"That's no hardship," he assured her.

"I also find it difficult when I'm naked and you're dressed."

"At times, I do that just so you are aware of your nudity. I think about what I'm doing at every step, Chelsea. If I'm dressed while you're naked, it's intentional, and I have a reason for it."

"I understand, Sir." And maybe she should be grateful, rather than pushing this. He was much less intimidating when he was clothed. She recalled his hot, muscular body, and rippled arm muscles. Yeah, much better if he stayed covered up.

"Is there anything specific you'd like to learn or spend time on?"

She was silent for a moment as she considered what she wanted to say. He expected her to reveal things that made her uncomfortable—that was part of the whole submission thing. She was accustomed to playing coy games with men, to teasing, to saying what they wanted to hear. But he'd proven he wanted much more than that from her.

"Chelsea?"

The knowledge that they would part after two weeks gave her confidence. It didn't matter what she said, since they wouldn't have a relationship going forward. The honesty demanded of a D/s left her a bit breathless. "I want to be able to endure whatever my Dom wants with confidence."

He moved across the room to pick up the hated collar.

"With your permission, I'd like to see how well you're doing on your postures."

She suppressed a shudder. "Of course, Sir."

He raised a questioning brow.

"I've been thinking, Sir. About this, about why I disliked it so much." She paused and pressed her lips together.

"I would like to understand," he said.

"Never mind." She sighed. Admitting this to him was just too embarrassing.

"Any insight you can share is helpful to me."

Just the sight of the black leather made coldness seep through her body. "It is more about the way you treated me than actually being restrained."

"The spanking? The tawse?"

"No." She shook her head. "I deserved that." She looked at him. She understood why he'd been such a big success in business, despite the Bartholomew deal, and why many of the firm's big clients had stayed with them. With the way he focused so intently, he had a way of making people feel listened to and heard. He didn't multitask. He gave his full attention. His gaze seemed to miss nothing. "It was the whole way you were..."

He waited in silence, holding the collar in one large hand.

"As if I meant nothing to you," she whispered. She glanced down and found a knot in the hardwood to focus on.

His touch gentle, he took her chin and tilted her head back. "Let me make this clear," he said. "I'm your trainer."

She nodded, feeling miserable.

"But I do not train subs unless I first like and respect them. If you sense distance from me, it is intentional. Doms are humans too, even male ones."

He cocked his head to one side in an apparent attempt at humour. She didn't smile. There was too much tension coiled in her for that.

Then he continued in the same serious vein. "We have failings. You may struggle with your feelings, and it's my job to help you manage your emotional state, as well as my own. For your sake *and* mine, I always compartmentalise punishment. It is serious business and needs to be honoured as such. I do not strike a sub with anger, but rather with deliberate intention. I want you to feel my punishment to reinforce your lessons. But I am always seeing to your safety first and foremost. Make no mistake, Chelsea. There is nothing, *nothing*, impersonal about this to me."

Hearing those words released some of the angst she'd been holding on to. She wanted this to mean as much to him as it did to her.

"Any questions?"

"No, Sir."

"Please, Chelsea, use your safe word or ask me to go slow if you need to. We can talk about anything at any time."

"Thank you, Sir. I think I am better now." And she wished she'd been able to discuss it with him earlier. Then again, she hadn't quite understood it herself. Submission was unchartered territory. Playing at parties was nothing like being with Master Alexander.

"When you're ready, stand and turn your back to me."

Conscious of the way he watched her so intently, she stood. Since he hadn't given instructions on what to do with her hands, she clenched them by her sides.

"Constricting any of your muscles will increase your mental discomfort. Uncurl your hands, Chelsea."

Did the man miss nothing?

"I'm going to tighten the collar more than last time, to keep your chin a bit more rigid."

Part of her wished he wouldn't tell her his intentions. She drew deep breaths as he fastened it, and she heard the sounds of his breathing, too.

When he was finished, he said, "Face me."

"Good." He took a step back to look at her. He adjusted her collar slightly and moved hair back from her forehead. "Come with me," he said.

He picked up the ever-present cane.

Curious, she followed him up the stairs and gripped the banister lightly to retain her equilibrium. She was more aware of her body than she'd ever been. With every step the plug jostled inside her. And the collar prevented her from looking around. The fact that she was nude made her feel overwhelmed. She moved slowly, and for some reason she'd never felt more feminine.

He led the way into the master bedroom. "Over there," he said, pointing and stepping aside.

A cheval mirror was angled in the corner. "Sir?"

"I want you to see what I do," he said.

Feeling somewhere between awkward and ridiculous, she moved towards the mirror. The room was reflected behind her, and she saw him drop the cane on the darkly masculine bedspread. "I don't get it, Sir."

He stood behind her and placed his hands on her shoulders.

Instead of looking at herself, she stared at his reflection. For the first time, she noticed a slight jagged scar above his right eyebrow.

"Look at how symmetrical your body appears with your head so straight and your shoulders back. See how open you appear. It's that juxtaposition. You appear more confident, which also makes you more appealing as a submissive."

She looked at her reflection and scowled. She noticed the flaws, the extra weight around her hips and the swell of her belly. "The mirror and I are not best friends, Sir," she said. She shook her head at her reflection. Generally she hurried through styling her hair, which consisted of scrunching the short, wet strands with a dollop of mousse. Then she slathered foundation on her face, applied a coat of mascara and walked away.

"Don't be critical," he said. "Be proud. Arch your back slightly so your chest sticks out further."

She did.

"Do you notice the difference?"

"That helps some," she said.

In the mirror, she saw him frown.

"Don't move," he said. He removed the collar. "Stand the way you usually do."

She shook out her arms, drew her feet closer together, and allowed her shoulders to roll forward. Her chin lowered a bit, too.

"Now look again."

"I get it." The difference shocked her. Standing up straight did add a confident air. Without being instructed, she moved around, lifting her head, drawing her shoulder blades together, spreading her legs for balance. The plug continued to remind her of its presence, but she no longer found it as annoying. In fact, on some level, it appealed to her. Wearing it pleased him.

"You're beautiful in your submission, Chelsea."

She wrinkled her nose.

"And arguing, even silently, doesn't become you."

"Sorry, Sir."

"I'm going to put the collar back on you, and you can watch the changes in the mirror."

Part of her felt as if it were punishment to have to look at herself the whole time. After seeing the set of his jaw, she remained silent.

"Smart girl," he said.

She was forced to lift her chin as he secured the collar and checked the fit. She had to admit that it made a difference in the way she stood.

"Now because of your aversion to looking at yourself, I will put you through your paces in front of the mirror. I want you to watch yourself and correct any flaws."

"Yes, Sir."

"Kneel up."

He stood to the side of her, cane held loosely in his right hand. She concentrated on each movement. The mirror made a huge difference, and she noticed that she was listing slightly to the left. She brought herself back to centre.

"Perfect," he said.

She met his gaze in the glass. He was impossibly handsome, but so different from men she had ever been attracted to before. She preferred men who were a bit smaller than he was. He must be six-foot-two, and it made her feel petite. She liked longer hair. And blond hair. She went for men with green or blue eyes, not the drownable brown like he had. Master Evan C was far more her type. So why did her heart quicken when she looked at Master Alexander?

"Inspect."

Since he didn't touch her, she knew he was just checking her positioning.

"Legs farther apart." With the cane, he tapped the inside of her right ankle. "Much better. Kneel up."

He made her go through every move no less than a dozen times. Through it all, she was aware of the dreaded plug's presence.

"Now stand with your hands folded loosely at your back." When she did, he asked, "Do you recall how you insisted you didn't want the cane to be used on your pussy?"

She shuddered. "You're not..." She couldn't get enough air into her lungs. "You mean that night, at the Den?" She had hoped, prayed that he had forgotten that. "You said you might punish my pussy with it."

"Tonight I'm going to show you it can be pleasurable."

When she looked in the mirror, the sight of him holding the cane filled her vision.

"I'm going to have you move through the positions again, but this time your wrists will be attached to the collar."

Did he say and do things in order to keep her guessing? She was expecting him to use the rattan on her, but instead he decided to cuff her.

He waited, obviously giving her time to protest or sort through things mentally. She bit the tip of her tongue. Arguing would be futile, she knew. When he was determined, he won. Because of her previous reaction to being restrained, she knew she had to repeat the lesson. That was certainly incentive to master something without complaint. "Anything you say, Sir." She wasn't quite sure how she kept the sarcasm out of her voice, but somehow she managed.

He placed the cane against the mirror where she couldn't help but see it. Clearly he had a sadistic streak. He walked into his closet and returned with cuffs. Within seconds, he had her wrists attached to the D-rings on her collar.

"Now, watch your reflection as you kneel back."

She was concentrating on him, and on what she was doing, so intently that the bondage didn't upset her this time.

"Well done," he said, when he'd had her stop in the inspect pose. "You were wobbly a couple of times, but since you couldn't use your hands for balance, you did better than I expected."

She grinned. "Thank you, Sir."

"Do you have a full-length mirror at home?"

"I do."

"Good. From here on, do your exercises in front of it."

Which meant making friends with the mirror, or at least not seeing it as an enemy. He didn't ask for much. "Of course, Sir."

He moved around her to pick up the cane. He stood next to the mirror, and she had to force herself not to take a step away or use her safe word.

"There's not as much room in here as I'd like. Please follow me to the guest room."

Walking behind him, she was very much aware of her submission. She tried to drop her head, but the collar prevented it.

The guest room was brightly lit. Other than a chair, there were no furnishings. A mirror adorned one wall, and there was a St Andrew's cross off to one side.

"Stand in the middle of the room, face me, and spread your feet as far as you can."

All of a sudden, her legs felt leaden. When she did as he said, he continued, "This may hurt a little," he told her. "If you fight it, it will hurt a lot."

She swallowed deep.

"But if you have the right attitude, you may enjoy it. Do you need to discuss anything?"

"Do I have to be wearing the collar?"

"I prefer it, yes. I want to keep your hands out of the way."

"So I can't protect my pussy?"

"You won't need to. Any further questions?"

"No. No, Sir," she amended.

He flicked his wrist a few times, and she heard a whistle as the rattan cut through the air. She flinched. "Sir, I don't think I've ever been more terrified in my life."

"You will never feel the full force of my cane against anything other than your legs or buttocks."

She wondered if those words were meant to reassure her. They didn't.

"Just as I require you to practise, I also take a few swings before hitting a sub."

"Uh. Thank you, Sir?"

"I use a different wrist motion when I use a cane or crop than I do when I swing a tawse or paddle. I never want to make a mistake and hit you somewhere I'm not intending."

"Thank God for that," she said.

"This particular cane is very whippy. I exercise all caution with it."

Part of her wished she'd played with one before. The fear of the unknown terrified her more than anything.

"Would you like an orgasm?"

"From that thing?" She scowled at the rattan.

"Ye of little faith," he mocked.

"I would like an orgasm, Sir. But I am sceptical."

"Moisten my fingers," he said.

She frowned.

"Stick out your tongue."

She complied without argument.

"Suck them," he said, voice sandpaper rough, when he put his fingers on her tongue.

He pulled away then moved his hand to her pussy. He slid his slickened fingers across her pussy until she helplessly jerked against his hand, then he entered her.

"Oh, Sir." She wanted to wrap her arms around him and hump him until she came.

"Not so quick."

All of the orgasm denial collided inside her, and tension built. Her legs trembled as she wordlessly sought more. He continued to play with her until she was within moments of coming. Then he stopped.

"Sir is an absolute beast," she said. She'd risen on her toes, and she slammed her heels to the ground.

"You'll earn it."

"I thought I already had, Sir."

"I'll decide that, sub."

He stepped back. "Let's see what a little slut you are, shall we?" He picked up the cane.

She was no longer feeling so aroused.

He brought the rattan between her legs. He tapped her clit.

"How's that?"

"Not as bad as I feared," she admitted.

"A little harder?"

"I'm not sure about that, Sir."

"We'll try it, shall we, hmm?"

He might have phrased it as a question, but she knew it was anything but. He stepped back a couple of inches and increased the pressure of the strokes. She cried out. Not from pain, but because she liked it. The fact she was restrained and helpless added to the delirium. "Sir, I'm really turned on," she admitted. "I need to come. Please? Please, may I?"

He didn't answer, and she jerked from the relentless hits.

"Sir? Master Alexander? I can't take any more. I swear. Please!"

Instead of allowing her to get off, frustratingly he moved the cane away, leaving her heaving, nerve endings singed.

She drank in several deep breaths.

"Do you have yourself under control?" he asked softly, about fifteen seconds later.

She met his gaze. She wished she could look down. Until he had introduced her to the posture collar, she'd had no idea how often she would glance at the floor to hide her emotions. "Yes, Sir."

"Good. You're doing very well. I'm proud of you. But there's more." He placed the length against her cunt. "Slide your pussy against the wood," he told her.

She had to bend her knees a bit to get enough pressure against the rattan. He wrapped one arm around her for support since her wrists were still attached to the collar. "This sounded easier in theory," she said, wrinkling her nose.

"I never said it was easy." He sounded surprisingly patient. "I just told you to do it. Hump the wood like the naughty slut you are. The way you did my hand. Now, get on with it."

It surprised her that she didn't feel mortified by his words. Instead, they liberated her. She was free to embrace her sexuality. In fact, he demanded it of her.

The wood was thin, and her damp pussy slid effortlessly along the waxed length. Despite her initial embarrassment, she ground herself against it, feeling herself getting wetter with each stroke. The sensations of the plug shifting inside her and dragging against the rattan magnified the feeling of being overwhelmed. Her breathing rate increased. And she heard his do the same. Rational thought was trampled by her physical desire. He tightened his grip around her, drawing her closer, lending more of his strength.

"That's it," he said encouraged.

The raspy sound of his voice against her ear drove her on. She'd never been with a man this masculine and demanding. She wanted more. She felt wild, wanton. Free. A climax built inside her again. "Sir, may I?" Keeping her balance became more and more difficult, and her whole body shook.

"Have you earned it?"

She was learning. "That's up to you to say, Sir. But I hope you'll think I have." Frantically, she moved back and forth.

He forced the wood against her even harder. The craving became desperation. She clenched her buttocks as she fought off the orgasm. "I beg you, Sir! Please, *please.*"

"Yes," he said.

His permission unshackled her. She jerked her body and sobbed. The slickness of her pussy and unyielding force of the cane collided, then gathered force. His voice encouraged her, his motions drove her.

"Come now," he ordered.

She shuddered desperately as the long-denied climax washed over her. She closed her eyes as she shook, a sensation of relief surrounding her. He continued to hold her, whispering reassuring words in her ear, and at some point, he pulled the cane away.

When she finally became aware of the world around her, the rattan was on the floor, and both of his arms enveloped her. She'd never felt safer, more secure or satiated.

"Let me get you out of this collar," he said.

"Thank you. Thank you for the orgasm, Sir." She wanted to remain where she was, as close to him as was possible with the collar. He set her away from him, but only far enough to release her arms. "Remember, slow. Rotate your shoulders. Give yourself a few moments to adjust."

Within a minute, he'd freed her. But instead of issuing a command as she expected, he drew her back against his chest. He dug one hand into her short hair and held her until her breathing returned to normal. The orgasm he'd given her was shattering, but she yearned for a deeper connection...for him. "Sir?"

"Hmm?"

"You mentioned giving head as part of my training, Sir."

He adjusted his stance and tipped back her chin. "We can do that tomorrow."

"I..."

"Tell me what you want, Chelsea."

"You'll think I'm ungrateful."

His lips quirked in a quick smile. "I'll be the judge of that."

The smile had transformed him, subtracting years and seriousness from his face. She caught a glimpse of the man he was before the perils of life had battered him. For a moment he'd looked carefree and a lot less stern. "I want sex," she admitted. "But you just brought me off."

"I will want you to leave the plug in."

She blinked. Nothing should shock her with him, but it did. "Is that even possible, Sir?"

"The fit will be tight. You'll either enjoy it or hate it."

"So it's not an option to remove the plug?"

"Afraid not."

She exhaled. The blasted thing was getting uncomfortable, and having his cock inside her would no doubt make it worse. "I'm willing to try, Sir."

He nodded. "Please crawl to the master bedroom."

She stood there, her mouth open.

He folded his arms implacably.

"Crawl?"

"I'm not repeating my command, Chelsea."

Silence stretched and tension became palpable. She reminded herself she had wanted to be the perfect sub. He waited without saying anything else. She knew she needed to make the first move. Feeling sort of mutinous, she gave an annoyed sigh and lowered herself to the floor.

"We'll practise crawling every day for a while," he said.

She should have figured as much. Why the hell didn't he just spank her and get it over with? In most of the fiction she'd read, stubborn or disobedient subs were summarily beaten. But he took a different, and unwelcome, approach.

"After you," he said.

She felt lewd, crawling in front of him down the hallway. The plug had to be clearly visible sticking out of her ass.

"Keep your head up," he told her. "You look sexy like this. A very good girl."

She wasn't feeling sexy. Though she was behaving as he instructed, her mind was rebellious. The sound of his shoes on the hardwood reminded her of her submission, and she disliked it.

In his bedroom, he looked at her. "Kneel up." He turned back the comforter and top sheet before ordering her onto the bed. "Lie on your back, across the mattress," he added. "And put your hands above your head."

She wondered about his instructions, but complied without question. She watched him undress, and he took little care with his clothes. He tossed his shoes towards the closet. His socks followed. He unbuttoned his shirt and hung it from the closet door.

Maybe she shouldn't have asked for this. She found it overwhelming when he was dressed and she was naked. But seeing his honed biceps reminded her of his power.

His gaze was on her as he unbuckled his belt and pulled the leather through the loops. For a wild, wicked moment she wondered what it would feel like if he used it on her.

"You'll find out," he said as if reading her mind.

Her mouth dried.

He dropped his trousers, and she saw he was wearing silk boxers. She'd never thought boxers were appealing, but on him they were totally masculine. When he removed them, she saw his cock was already hard. She wasn't sure she'd ever seen a man who was so broad and honed.

She parted her legs and expected him to enter her. Instead, he knelt over her.

"Suck my dick, sub."

Oh, Lord. He loomed above her and filled her vision with his ball sac and erect cock.

She'd never done anything like this and feelings of helplessness slammed into her.

Because he had leverage, he could have choked her, but he initially only shoved his cockhead inside her mouth.

"Take a little more," he said.

She started to move her hands so she had a little control, but he ensnared her wrists.

She licked and sucked him, trying not to focus on how big he was and how totally he filled her.

"Good girl."

When he groaned, she redoubled her efforts to please him. He jerked his hips, going deeper down her throat, claiming dominion over her.

By the time he pulled out, she was gasping and choking, feeling surrendered and no longer able to think.

"That will do. For now."

At first, she'd done okay, but towards the end, physical sensation had swamped her. And the sound of his voice told her he'd been as into it as she was.

He moved off the bed and she swiped the back of her hand across her mouth.

She saw him grab a condom from the top drawer of the nightstand. Her pussy moistened in anticipation as she watched him. His cock was thick and red, and she spread her legs a bit more in anticipation.

Before he sank into her, he teased her clit. "You're slick for me, Chelsea," he said, and she heard the approval in his voice.

"I think you're sexy, Sir."

"I think you're almost ready." He knelt and wrapped his arms around her thighs to drag her closer to his face. "Only fair," he said.

He licked her cunt and she arched her back. "Sir!"

"No coming without permission." He played with the base of the plug, tapping on it and pulling it out a little before releasing it.

"Oh, Sir! I am ready to come."

"Soon," he promised. "But not yet."

He inserted a finger in her, then a second. She grabbed hold of the sheet, digging in her fingers as she tried to stave off the orgasm.

When she was thrashing her head back and forth, he finally stopped and stood.

"Sir, fuck me."

"Scoot back."

He helped her towards the middle of the bed, then he moved between her legs. He pressed his thumb against her clit as he pushed the tip of his cock inside her. She clenched his forearms. As he eased in, the plug filled her insides, making the fit of his dick impossibly tight. "I'm not sure I can manage, Sir."

"Try for me," he said as he went in deeper.

She cried out. She had never felt anything so intense.

"Wrap your legs around my waist."

The pressure had her paralysed, and she wasn't sure she could follow his instructions, no matter how much she wanted to. He moved slightly so that he could lift her hips.

"Now do it," he said.

With his support, she was able to do as he asked. With her spread helplessly, he claimed her pussy. She cried out.

"Chelsea?"

"I'm okay. I... Wow. So tight, Sir."

"Would you like me to stop?"

She looked at him, and admitted her darkest desires. "No. I'd like you to fuck me."

He gave a nod indicating his approval. Her heart soared.

"I asked you to keep your hands above your head."

She felt colour drain from her face. "Sorry, Sir." She put them where they were supposed to be, and he pinned her wrists to the mattress. His grip was firm and seductive. Her insides tightened.

"That's better," he said.

"Do me, Sir."

"My pleasure, girl."

This moment, with him poised over her, was everything she'd wanted. The feeling of being compliant and wanted turned her inside out.

He slid into her again, and she was shocked by how slick she was, how ready for him.

"Yeah," he said on a groan.

Master Alexander pulled out slightly, then re-entered her.

She was lost. "More," she said, asked, demanded.

He fucked her slowly at first, building the intensity in her. She thrashed her head as he stroked her insides with his thick cock. "Yes," she said.

He rode her harder and harder.

"You're right," he said, his voice sounding guttural. "You feel tight. You're a hot little submissive. *Fuck*."

Pure feminine pleasure bloomed. This man was always so controlled, and clearly the sex was affecting him, too. Yes.

"Come," he said. "Anytime."

She closed her eyes as he did her. Because of the unique internal pressure it was more difficult for her to achieve orgasm than a few minutes ago. These sensations made her delirious.

He pistoned his hips, driving deeper.

"Sir... Master Alexander..." She didn't know what she was asking. The only thing she knew was that she couldn't survive much more.

Finally a climax overtook her, but not in a way it ever had before. This started somewhere deep inside her and eased its way up, long and sustained.

When she thought it would remain frustratingly out of reach, it overtook her. She struggled against his hold, reaching for more.

He moaned as her pussy muscles squeezed him.

"So damn hot," he said. He lifted his body. "Look at me."

She opened her eyes.

His eyes were darker than she'd ever seen them, and he seemed to stare straight into her. Fancifully, she wondered if he could see all her secrets.

He jerked his hips, creating shallow motions in her. Absolutely. There was no doubt, this Dom was attuned to her enough to know everything about her. He kept his gaze focused on her, reading her reactions. With perfect timing, he forced another orgasm from her. She cried out, never having been more satisfied.

"Chelsea..."

"Come in me, Sir."

Unbelievably he held back, waiting until after she had another orgasm. Her breaths were shallow and ragged. She wasn't sure how much more she could take. Several more seconds passed before he froze. "Sir," she whispered.

He shuddered, then she felt the tell-tale pulse of his cock as he ejaculated. He filled the condom and bit the side of her neck.

She felt owned, possessed, happy.

For a moment, he collapsed on her, making it impossible for her to completely fill her lungs. But she didn't protest. She liked having him inside her, enjoyed his possession. Master Alexander made her feel ultra-feminine.

She wrestled her arms from his grip and threaded the fingers of one hand into his hair. She ran her other hand down his back. Under his tutelage, she was changing. She had never been the nurturing type, but he made her want to soothe him. The impulse made her smile. She was a woman, and he was a big, bad Dom.

After a few moments, he shifted their positions so that she was on her side and he was behind her. He held her tight. She stiffened momentarily.

"Shh. Fight me in five minutes. For now, enjoy."

He doesn't ask for much. She fought the impulse to get out of bed and go home, anything to put some distance between them.

"You can do it willingly, Chelsea, or I can tie you to the headboard and force you to let me snuggle you. Either way, I win."

To reinforce his words, he drew her closer. Five seconds later, he pinched her buttock. She squealed and jerked. He settled her even closer to him.

"Fine," she said.

"Fine?"

"I mean, thank you, Sir." The man terrified her. If she gave him the time he demanded, she was afraid she'd never want to leave.

His arm was draped across her, and she was reminded how big he was. He placed a hand right above her pelvic bone and inched her backwards so that her rear was curved against him. She was aware of the plug still, and his semi-flaccid cock. This was more intimacy than she usually allowed. It bothered her that she liked it.

True to his word, he didn't imprison her for long. He released her and climbed from the bed. "Move it," he said, coming around to the side she was facing. "Into the bathroom so I can take out the plug."

For some reason, that sounded like a threat.

"Do you have an objection, sub?"

She sorted through her feelings. "This may be ridiculous, but the idea bothers me."

"I fucked you with it."

"I know. But... I don't know. That seems more personal than what we did earlier, Sir."

"Let go of your need to control everything."

She curled into a tighter ball.

He scooped her from the bed. She gasped and held onto him so he wouldn't drop her.

He strode into the en suite bathroom and continued to hold her, for far longer than necessary. "This is amazing," she said. She'd never seen anything like this in a private home. He had to have knocked down walls to create such a large, spa-like space.

The tile floor was black and white in art deco style. A claw-foot tub stood off to one side. An extra-large shower had benches built in and dual showerheads on poles. The water closet was behind another door, and there were two sinks with tall, arched faucets. Shelves held candles and numerous decorator touches. A skylight completed the space.

"Get on all fours, forehead on the floor," he said, sliding her down his body "You may use the rug."

"I'm going to die of humiliation," she protested as she stepped away from him.

"Not likely. But you are going to get a beating if you stall one more second."

"Yes, Sir." Mortification eating her from the inside out, she lowered herself as he'd ordered and presented her ass to him. She squeezed her eyes shut as he pulled out the long piece of silicone.

She heard him drop it in the sink.

"That wasn't so bad, was it?" he asked.

Her ass burned for a moment, then the pain faded instantly. Where the plug had felt invasive, she now felt vaguely empty.

"Your ass is nicely stretched. I'm looking forward to the opportunity to fuck you up there. Please stand."

She did, and she met his gaze.

"You've pleased me very much."

"Thank you, Sir."

Are you still determined to go home tonight?"

She nodded.

"Shower, first," he said, turning on the faucet.

Another first. She'd never showered with a man before. He checked the water temperature then pushed her inside the stall.

"You're going to let me do this, so I suggest you don't even start an argument."

She shut her mouth as he adjusted the water's height so it hit her shoulders. Beneath the spray, tension left her body.

He then removed the other showerhead from its pole and directed the spray down her body.

"Turn around."

He soaped her skin, lathering her with one motion and rinsing her with the next.

She tensed when he rinsed between her buttocks. "Sir, this is really personal."

"Yes, sub. It is."

Apparently unconcerned by her protests, he continued.

Since it didn't appear to bother him, she forced herself to relax.

"Better," he approved. "Maybe you'll get the hang of this submission thing. Now, face me again."

He washed her breasts, her abdomen, her belly, even her legs. "I thought I was supposed to do this for you, Sir."

"At times," he agreed. "But caring for a sub's needs is part of being a good Dom."

He was right. If this continued and he pampered her like this all the time, she would most assuredly get the hang of this submission thing.

When he was done washing her, he grabbed a towel that he'd thrown over the top rack and dried her. He took exquisite care of her, drying each part of her, even between her legs.

She realised she shouldn't be so stubborn. She could stay the night, curled up in his inviting bed. But she knew herself too well. If she yielded, it would be too easy to start caring for him.

He allowed her to keep the towel wrapped around her as she followed him down the stairs. Unfortunately, he'd donned a loose-fitting pair of athletic pants and a T-shirt. He still looked every bit as hot as he did naked, though.

As she dressed, he said, "There's a party a week from Saturday night at the Den. I understand Evan C will be in attendance."

Excitement and anticipation thrummed through her at his words. She'd sent the confounded man several e-mails and even an unsolicited proposal for his career. She'd received nothing back but an automatic response saying that he appreciated her writing to him and, due to the large volume of correspondence he received, he regretted he was unable to send a personal reply. Which was exactly why he needed to hire her. He didn't realise how many more sales he could generate if he had a strategic social networking plan. His refusal to acknowledge his fans was career suicide.

This was the opportunity she'd been working towards. She might not be the world's most fabulous submissive yet, but she had made significant improvements since she'd seen him last. She was sure to get his attention.

And she still had some time left to refine her skills.

"Would you like to go?" Master Alexander asked.

Her heart quickened. Everything she'd worked for was coming together. "You'll take me, Sir?"

"If you'd like a companion. Otherwise, you can go alone. I'm sure Master Damien will add you to the party list. It's a perfect opportunity for you to show what you've learnt. It's your call. But if you'd like, I'd be honoured to accompany you."

Chapter Seven

Alex folded his arms and looked down at the naked Chelsea. She was at his home for the fifth day in a row. Every time she showed up, her behaviour was more and more perfect. He knew she'd joined some online communities where she was getting feedback from other submissives, and it showed.

She occasionally set her chin in a mutinous line, but those occasions were becoming rarer. He still put her in a posture collar from time to time, but she had ceased protesting that, also. Today she was naked, except for a pair of stockings and heels she referred to as 'stupid high'. He thought they were almost tall enough.

He knew she was looking forward to having the opportunity to see Master Evan C. And it seemed her efforts to learn everything possible had redoubled when he'd invited her to the upcoming party at the Den. "Present your breasts, sub."

"Yes, Sir," Chelsea said, her voice strong. At his request, she never whispered now. She lifted her breasts and drew them together. She looked at the floor the whole time.

If he had a sub, he'd want her to be just like Chelsea. "Ask me to clamp your nipples." This was the first time he'd asked that of her, and he wondered how she would respond.

"Please, Sir, clamp my nipples as hard as you want."

He pinched the rosy tips, and she winced. He tugged hard, and she moaned but didn't protest.

"Thank you, Sir," she said when he released her.

"These are Japanese clovers," he told her. A sturdy chain ran between each clamp, and he dangled it over his index finger. He held them in front of her eyes so they filled her vision. "I've selected a fairly vicious pair." He saw her shoulders tighten. "But if you learn with these, others will be very easy to tolerate."

"If you say so, Sir."

He squeezed her left nipple hard, then closed a clamp over it.

"*Jesus*, Sir!"

"I take it that hurts."

"I want it off." She glared at him

"Then use your safe word or figure out how to change your attitude and compartmentalise the pain."

She breathed in. Despite her obvious discomfort and the anger he heard in her voice, she continued to hold her breasts for his torture. She was learning. "Good girl."

At his words, she exhaled a shaky breath.

More than any other woman he'd been with, she responded the most favourably to his approval. A few words from him had the ability to change her attitude. "Now you pinch your other nipple."

"Sir is an absolute..." She trailed off.

"Good thing you didn't finish that sentence," he said into the silence. "You will be punished for saying that much, though."

She stuck out her lower lip.

"And for that attempt at manipulation."

"I…" She sighed. "I apologise."

"Please don't. It's been a while since you felt my wrath. I'm looking forward to reinforcing my rules." Although she sometimes got off when he used corporal punishment on her, she was so different from Liz. Chelsea liked pain, but she didn't crave it like an addict did a fix. The idea of relinquishing her to another Dom, especially one who was unworthy, pissed him off. But hadn't he had his fill of keeping a woman he'd taken in for training? "Pinch that nipple." He looked at her and waited for her reaction. She blinked several times but said nothing. He gave the chain a fast yank.

She screamed.

"Pinch your nipple," he repeated. "Hold it for five seconds and then release it."

The moment she did, he clamped her nipple. Her breaths were ragged, but she remembered to keep her breasts cupped. "You really are becoming a well-behaved submissive."

"Thank you, Sir."

"At times," he amended. "You may let go of your breasts."

She remembered to express her gratitude again.

He gathered the metal chain in his fist. "The reason these are my favourites is that when you tug on them, they tighten, rather than coming off." To show her what he meant, he said, "Stand." He exerted pressure on her tits as she climbed to her feet in a shaky move. He did love the sight of her calves in the stilettos.

Once she found her footing, he tugged again, urging her onto her tiptoes. "I should have clamped you a long time ago. It works great as a leash."

"Sir! Fuck!"

"Over here," he said, leading her to the couch.

She had no choice but to follow, but she didn't question him.

"Kneel up." He released the chain, and the sudden change in tension made her wince again.

When she had settled into position, he said, "Remove my belt."

"Are you…"

"Going to punish you? Yes."

Her lower lip trembled, but he knew this time it was from fear, rather than an attempt to sway him.

She unfastened his buckle, then slid the leather through the loops. "You're staying dressed, Sir?"

"You told me that it reinforces your subservience. So yes. I want you to be aware of your station."

"Of course." She doubled the leather over and held it.

"Offer it to me."

She extended her hands and looked at the floor.

"I like the way you do that. It's incentive to punish you more."

She shuddered as she returned to the kneel up position. He sat on the couch. "Over my lap, girl." To hurry her along, he grabbed the chain.

"I'm coming, Sir."

"Was that hostility in your tone?"

"No, Sir."

She draped herself across his lap. He jostled her around slightly. "If you need to grab hold of my ankles for support, you may. But you may not try to evade what you have coming to you."

"I understand."

"I'm going to give you eight strokes."

"Thank you, Sir."

He rubbed her skin to get the blood flowing. If she were his, he would enjoy seeing marks that lasted, but he was aware she probably wanted to look good for Master Evan C. "How do your nipple clamps feel?"

"Fine, Sir."

"I could put weights on the chain if you need a bit more pressure."

"I think they're sufficiently evil as they are, Sir."

He grinned. She sounded prim and proper. "Are you ready for your spanking, Chelsea?"

"Yes, Sir. And before you get started, I do promise to watch my mouth more in future."

"Good plan," he approved. He swung the belt hard, catching her across both butt cheeks at the same time.

She yelped, but she said, "Thank you, Sir."

After the second, she lifted her head slightly but thanked him again.

For her training, he'd been concentrating on the small details of submission, tone of voice, pretty motions, anal penetration, bondage, and posture. She took his belt well.

He traced her spine—mainly because he enjoyed touching her—before he laid the leather to her again.

Chelsea arched in response to the blow, but didn't protest.

He applied more pressure to the fourth stroke.

She grunted, a very unladylike sound, but otherwise, she remained quiet. She would definitely please some future Dom. "Move forwards a bit," he told her. "Palms flat on the floor. I want to give the backs of your thighs some attention."

When she hesitated, he dropped his left knee a bit to tip her off balance.

He finished the punishment, belting her several times in rapid succession.

She hadn't protested even once, and when he tossed the strap aside, she said, "That was hot, Sir. Thank you."

"It was meant as punishment, not pleasure," he said.

"It did hurt," she said.

Was she trying to reassure him? His lips quirked. He intended to teach her a lesson, but if she'd liked it as well, he could live with that. "Present, lying down on the floor."

She moved quicker than he thought she might. Oh, yes, she was pleasing.

He bent to rub a finger up the inside of her pussy lips. With a frown, he asked, "Did you shave this morning?"

"No. It was last night, Sir."

"It feels as if it's been several days. Take a little more care next time."

Her thighs quivered. "Sorry, Sir."

He slapped her cunt hard.

She screamed.

"That's a gentle reminder." He'd hit her hard enough to drive his lesson home and to ensure she wouldn't think it was meant as a turn-on.

"I won't be so remiss next time, Sir."

He believed her. He wouldn't be surprised if she started keeping a razor at the office. "How do those clamps feel now?"

"They're starting to burn, Sir."

"Shall I distract you?"

"Please."

He toyed with her pussy. She shifted beneath his hand.

"Oh my…"

"Yes?"

"Sir, that's…"

"Go on."

"The pain in my nipples is making me more aroused than I could imagine."

"Not so bad now, Chelsea?"

"It's exquisite, Sir. With my ass throbbing, too, it's… Oh, God, I want to come!"

She became slicker. Shamelessly she pushed her pelvis against his hand. He debated whether or not he'd let her come. She'd been punished, and she'd been a little sloppy in her shaving. "I can smell you."

"Please, Sir. Please," she called out. "May I come?"

He moved his hand away. "I think that's enough for today."

"But—"

"Enough."

She closed her eyes and grimaced in apparent irritation.

"You can suck my dick to thank me for putting up with such an ill-mannered trainee," he said.

"Thank you, Sir."

She crawled over to him and unbuttoned his trousers. They fell around his ankles. She worked her hand inside his boxers and stroked his cock, making it hard before she removed those, too. Spanking her, smelling her, hearing her moans of need, had made him horny.

She looked up at him through her eyelashes, one of the most seductive things he'd ever seen. She cradled his balls and ran her thumb over the slit in his cock to transfer the first drop of pre-ejaculate onto her skin then into her mouth. She made a show of sucking her thumb.

He captured the chain that ran between her nipples. "Let's make this more interesting," he said. He pulled her up onto her knees and looped the linked metal over his hard cock. It would prevent her from pulling too far away.

"Ah... Diabolical, Sir," she said.

"Don't touch yourself," he warned.

Chelsea set to work giving him head, keeping her mouth open wide to take as much of him as his thrusts demanded. She sucked him, licking his cockhead. He dug his hands into the short waves of her hair, cradling her skull and holding her prisoner.

He rocked his hips until he found the rhythm he wanted, then he held her head tighter so he could fuck her mouth. "You're doing well."

She made slight gagging sounds, something they'd need to work on correcting, but she continued to service him. Of course, with the way he was holding her and the way the chain dragged on her nipples, she had little choice.

"Swallow every drop when I come."

She nodded as much as possible. He tipped back his head and closed his eyes, enjoying the feeling of having his dick down her throat. Absently he wondered why he'd been so adamant about not playing with subs. Being with a woman who was so desperate to please was the stuff of dreams.

Her enthusiasm increased as his cock thickened. Need boiled from deep in his balls. "Every drop," he warned before he could no longer speak.

He groaned as hot cum pulsed into her mouth.

Dutifully she worked to take the load, swallowing, licking.

He immobilised her head as she sucked him dry.

When she was done, she tried to kneel back, but the pain in her nipples forced her back upright.

"I may do that to you every time you give me head."

"Yeah, about that, Sir..." She wiped the back of her hand across her mouth. "I liked sucking your dick, Sir," she said. "Thank you."

"You did well. How wet is your cunt?"

"Not very," she said.

"You're no longer on the verge of coming?"

She shook her head, then stilled as the chain moved.

His cock became flaccid, and he dropped her chain. She winced a little.

"You may get dressed."

"Sir?" She blinked, looking up at him.

"That's enough for tonight. Get dressed, but leave the clamps on. Do not remove them until you arrive home."

She opened her mouth as if to protest, but then closed it without saying a word.

"Very wise," he said. He pulled up his boxers and pants, zipping and buttoning them as she wiggled into her skirt and thong. He folded his arms as he watched her shrug into her blouse. Her movements were careful, in deference to the clamps, and she left off her bra entirely. "Call me when you get home for permission to remove the clamps."

"Yes, Sir."

She gathered her belongings, removed her keys from the hook inside her purse, then stuffed her bra in the shallow depths. He walked her to her car and tugged on the chain as she slid the key into the ignition.

"Do you show no mercy?" she asked.

"Would you like to sleep in them?"

"Thank you for your generosity in letting me remove them when I get home, Sir."

"I would have hated to give you a bare-assed spanking right here in front of the neighbours. I'm sure Mr Jones across the street would enjoy the view."

She gasped. "You wouldn't."

"Try me. I'll have you over that hood with your skirt around your waist so fast you won't remember your name."

She sank deeper into the leather seat.

"Drive safe," he said, flicking the door closed.

He watched until she accelerated away then turned the corner. She had looked in the rear view mirror a couple of times, but she hadn't waved.

And he realised why he didn't play with subs more often. He had discriminating tastes. And he wanted a sub like her.

Less than half an hour later, she called.

"I'm home, Sir. Thank you for an instructive evening."

"How do your nipples feel?"

"Numb."

"They won't be when you take off the clamps."

"I'm sure you're right."

"Let's find out. Put your phone on speaker so you don't have to hold it, then remove your shirt." He heard rustling sounds that indicated she was following his directions.

"Damn. Every little motion hurts, Sir."

"Good. Good. You're being very obedient."

"I'm putting my shirt in the laundry hamper."

Of course she would put it where it belonged.

"I'm removing the right clamp now, Sir."

She gasped. "Fuck. Fuck, fuck, fuck, fuck, *fuck*."

He imagined sucking on the tip. It might hurt initially, but the hurt would soon vanish. She'd be writhing beneath him in no time. Even though she'd sucked him off less than an hour ago, his cock responded to the sound of her pain. "Now the other one."

"Damn. I wish there was a way to get this off without it hurting."

"Then you'd defeat my purpose."

"You want me to suffer," she said.

"Oh, yes, my sweet girl. All the time. Take it off. Now."

She whimpered.

"You're stalling."

"Yes." There was silence followed by a loud hiss. It took her a few seconds before she said, "Damn."

"Too bad I didn't put one on your clit."

"Thank you for your kindness."

"You still need work on your manners."

"I'll be honest, Sir. It's hard to remember when I hurt so bad. It's like everything is in a haze. I can hardly think."

"When you're instructed to do something, you may want to think it all the way through. Break it down in your mind, first. For example, tell yourself you'll remove the clamp and immediately express your gratitude. Think how much your Dom wants to hear those words. There are many things he or she could be doing other than listening to your complaints."

"You're right, Sir. I beg your pardon."

"You're going to be tempted to masturbate tonight," he said. "Your breasts and nipples will be sensitive, and with the way I played with your cunt earlier, you'll want to come. But I forbid it. You didn't earn it, and it doesn't matter how wrong you think I am. Do not pleasure yourself."

He remained silent until she said, "I understand, Sir."

"When you arrive tomorrow, I want you wearing the clamps." He pictured her gritting her teeth to hold back a disrespectful response. He was pushing her limits now, and he knew it.

"Anything else, Sir?"

"That will be all, Chelsea. I will let you know if I change my mind." And he might.

"I was wondering…"

"Go on."

"Saturday is the day after tomorrow. Can we spend some extra time together? I know you're busy, but I was hoping you could beat me."

"You know what you're asking?"

"Master Evan C likes to tie up his subs and whip them."

Alex nodded. She was right about that. "Does early afternoon work for you? I'd like to take you to out to dinner to give you a little more exposure to being in public."

"I'll rearrange my schedule. Three o'clock all right with you, Sir?"

"It is. Make sure you have heels and a skirt. Look at your rear in the mirror. If there are any welts, put arnica on them. Oh, and there is one more thing for tonight. Sleep in the nude." He didn't give her time to respond. He pressed the icon to end the conversation, then he went back downstairs and poured himself a whisky. Generally, she tried to negotiate a later start to their evening, but now that time with Evan C was looming, she wanted more practice. Evan C, if he weren't such a prick, would realise he was a lucky man.

Honouring her request for tomorrow's session, he headed back upstairs to prepare the guest room. He moved the St Andrew's cross into the middle of the room, and he selected two floggers. If she wanted a beating, he'd give her one. The first flogger would warm her nicely. The second would satisfy her desire to experience a real whipping.

He looked forward to using both.

Even though he'd forbidden Chelsea to touch herself, he climbed beneath the hot shower spray and jacked off to the image of her on her knees, the clamp's chain hooked over his thick cock as she sucked him deep into her mouth.

The next day, at two minutes before three o'clock, he heard a car door slam. As always, she was right on time. About thirty seconds later, she knocked on his front door. He had told her she didn't need to, but she did, regardless.

There was a metallic creak as she opened the front door, then a soft *snick* as she closed it behind her. He heard the faint staccato of her heels against the hardwood floors. Presumably she was making her way into the living room. Then there was silence.

Over their days together, he'd discovered he liked having her here. He enjoyed her company, and he liked knowing she was preparing for him, stripping off her clothes and folding them in a perfect pile. He resisted the impulse to hurry to her. Instead decided to finish work on his third-quarter financial projections.

She still tended to get impatient after only a couple of minutes, so he kept her waiting. He'd left lights on downstairs so she knew he was home. He had done what he needed to reassure her she wasn't alone. The rest was up to her.

Alex had been a trainer for years. It was customary for him to spend days or weeks with a submissive then send her back to her Dom. Her enthusiasm to be perfect for Evan C shouldn't have surprised Alex, after all, that was why she'd pursued him.

What did surprise him was the way he reacted to her.

There was something rewarding about making her surrender, giving up the control she liked to exert. And the way she responded to him in bed... A transformation came over her when she ceased the struggle. In bed, she was unrestrained. He'd never been with a woman so responsive and so vocal about it.

Each time he'd inserted a plug up her tight ass, she'd protested, but when he fucked her with it in, she screamed out her orgasms. When they had sex, her hot pussy enveloped him, and more than once over the last couple of days, the way she'd squeezed him had dragged his ejaculate from him sooner than he liked. The little vixen wasn't the only one swamped by physical need.

But it was more than that. She was passionate about all her pursuits. Since he'd met her, she'd sent a number of e-mails reinforcing her suggestion that Monahan Capital host a charity function. Of course, she suggested her firm handle the event. Each solicitation contained a new suggestion or reason, so he knew she was always thinking about his business. She'd been so persistent—and convincing—that he'd considered approaching his brother with the idea. He figured she was such a success in business because she refused to take no for an answer. Which pretty well meant he and Evan C were both done for.

After Alex did a check sum on each calculation, he closed the spreadsheet then pushed back from his desk. He hadn't got a lot done this morning, despite his best intentions. Thoughts of Chelsea had dominated his mind. He went downstairs, and he found her in the kneeling up position, with the clover clamps biting into her nipples. "You're doing well," he told her. After the party, in fact, there wouldn't be any reason to continue her training. He'd got her comfortable with anal. Her movements were pleasing. And for the most part, she followed direction without argument. She even sucked cock well. He didn't like the thought, so he ruthlessly shoved it away. "Have you climaxed since you left here last night?"

"You forbade it, Sir."

"Answer the question, Chelsea."

"That was my answer," she said. "I do not go behind your back, Sir, no matter how tempted I am. So, no. I did not come."

Her answer pleased him, ridiculously so. "Crawl upstairs to the guest room," he instructed.

"Of course, Sir."

She lowered herself to the floor with elegance that proved she'd continued to hone her skills even when they were apart. She managed to navigate each wooden step without protest. "Very nice," he said as he followed her down the hallway.

"Thank you, Sir."

She didn't ask him to remove the clamps, and with the way her body swayed, he knew she had to hurt. She moved a little slower as she crossed the threshold into the room and obviously saw the cross. "Keep going. I want you on the cross, facing away from me."

When she reached the sturdy base, she stood and spread her arms and legs wide, into the shape of an X.

He secured her limbs then walked in front of the cross. He captured her chin. "How are the clamps?"

"Miserable, Sir."

"Would you like me to remove them?"

She opened her eyes wide and searched his gaze. "If it pleases you, Sir."

"If I were giving you an erotic beating, I might request you leave them on as they would heighten your arousal in the event I let you come. For now, I'm all right with you concentrating on the flogging. So I will leave the choice to you."

"In that case, Sir, I'd appreciate it if you got rid of the nasty little beasts."

"Chelsea, Chelsea, Chelsea."

"Thank you, Sir." She smiled at him.

He knew she didn't mean it to be manipulative, but it was. He liked the sight of her smile so much he'd allow her to get away with almost anything just to see it. He captured her right breast in his palm and squeezed the flesh before releasing the clamp.

She sucked in a shallow breath. And he bent to soothe the hurt with his mouth.

Her body trembled, but when he released her, she said, "Well, Sir. That was certainly better than when I took them off last night. Thank you for making it much more pleasurable."

"Ready for the next one?"

"Please."

He squeezed the other breast and plucked the clamp from the tip. He licked and teased the nipple until her breathing returned to normal.

"Sir, I know you don't want me getting aroused, but...uhm, I am."

After he released her, he slid two fingers between her legs. "You are damp, little pain slut."

"I..." She trailed off and moved her hips towards him, as much as the rigid constraint of the wood would allow.

He continued to rub her, back and forth, across her clit.

"Sir, may I come?" She pulled against her bonds.

"Having your nipples clamped made you this wet?"

"Oh, Sir. Yes. No."

He slid a finger inside her, pulled out again.

"Yes, it was from the clamps. But it was also because of last night's spanking with your belt. And the way you smacked my pussy. I hardly slept last night because I wanted to have sex with you. I woke up thinking about you."

He told himself that only meant she wanted to get off. But his ego wanted her to crave satisfaction from him.

"I've been obsessed with imagining what today would be like," she confessed.

She struggled, and he couldn't tell whether it was to get away, to avoid orgasming without permission or whether she was trying to get him to use more pressure. He saw her digging her toes into the hardwood floor.

"Sir! I'm begging you. Please, please stop. If you keep doing that, I'm going to be helpless. And I don't want to displease you."

"Come, Chelsea." He grabbed one of her nipples and pinched brutally. "Now."

"Oh, thank you, Sir." She convulsed against the straps, her pussy constricting as she came.

He released his grip on her nipple, and she sobbed words of gratitude. He reached to smooth his thumb across the top of her eyebrows. "You are so responsive," he told her.

"It's you who turns me on and keeps me there, Sir. And I wanted to tell you how much I enjoyed sucking your cock last night. You keep trying to get me to give up control, and when I don't, you seize it. I find that so...masculine. You make me happy to be a woman, Sir, and I like it," she said. She nipped at his hand and when she managed to get hold of the fleshy part at the base, she held on with her teeth.

He wasn't sure he'd felt anything more sexy. In the only physical way she had available, she reached out to him.

Yeah. Evan C was one lucky sonofabitch.

Once she released him, he placed his palms on either side of her face. "Do you still want to continue with a flogging?"

"I do. Being on this structure is mind-blowing. I wasn't sure how I'd like it, since I hated the posture collar. At first, I mean."

He nodded.

"But I think I'm finally starting to understand what you meant from the start. I am freer to explore my own reactions when I'm restrained. I can fight, but I can't get away. With the wrong person, it could be scary. With you it's not." Then she added, "Thank you."

"There's still more," he said.

She gave him what had to be an intentional, sly smile. "I'm ready, Sir."

He left her for a moment and returned with one of the floggers he'd selected in advance. "You'll notice this one has fairly thick strands. It will make a thuddy kind of impact. As far as floggers go, it's considered quite innocuous. Do keep in mind, how it's wielded makes all the difference."

"You showed me that when you used the cane on me, Sir."

"Precisely. Where I hit, the force behind my wrist, where I stand, all of it factors into your corresponding pain." He shook out the leather.

She looked at it with an expression of curiosity rather than fear.

"If I wanted to beat you for half the night until you went into subspace, I'd choose this one for you." And maybe he should. He'd had no idea she would respond so favourably to pain. "After I've warmed up your skin, I'll switch to a different one." He exchanged the floggers and returned to her. "This is one of several I use for punishment, or for a very experienced sub who enjoys impact play. I want to be clear that you're neither being punished, nor do I consider you anything other than a novice." He flicked his wrist. He smelt leather and heard a sound like a distant waterfall. He'd forgotten how much he liked holding this type of whip. "I am introducing you to its feel. If you'll notice, the leather strands are thinner so it results in a powerful sting. Would you like to use your safe word?"

Chelsea licked her upper lip before responding, "No, Sir."

He noticed she hadn't taken her gaze off the whip.

"Any questions?"

"Can we get on with it, Sir?"

"You do like to tempt fate."

She grinned. "In for a penny," she said. "Then I'll tell you I think you look hot, Sir."

His cock hardened. This morning he had dressed for his time with Chelsea. Instead of his customary business attire, he'd worn a short-sleeved T-shirt, black jeans, and motorcycle boots.

"Leather pants would be better," she continued. "Do you have any? Could you wear them tomorrow?"

"I will choose my attire, girl. And yours."

"Of course, Sir. Did you get my e-mail yesterday? I thought we could use the grounds of the Den as a setting for a photo shoot. Pictures of you in those pants and maybe a hat like you wore that first night... That would be good for your image. With the mountains as a backdrop you'll look more well-rounded."

He resisted a smile. This woman definitely liked to be in control, even when she was helpless, affixed to bondage equipment. "Monahan Capital has its own PR firm," he reminded her, reminded them both. "And I'm not running for political office."

"I sent you a proposal yesterday—"

"Would you like to wear a dental dam?" he interrupted.

"Shutting up, Sir."

"Good choice. In that case, we'll get on with it." He crossed the room and placed the flogger with the first. He went to her for a moment and trailed his touch over her body. "If you can, let some of the tension out of your muscles." He pressed his body against hers and uncurled her fists. "That's better," he said. "Splaying your fingers will keep your muscles more supple."

Being this close to her wasn't a good idea. When he drew in the scent of her shampoo and layered floral soap, he had a very masculine reaction. He wanted to be buried in her cunt, or her ass, and claim her as his. *Fuck.* Where the hell had that thought come from?

"Oh, Sir," she said on a moan. "Do me?"

He moved away and grabbed the flogger. "A Dom's cock has to be earned, Chelsea." He hoped she didn't hear the gruffness in his tone.

"Then I'll do whatever I need to in order to deserve having your cock in me, Sir."

If the angle weren't nearly impossible, he'd drop his jeans and ride her now.

He took a few moments to mentally centre himself. He refused to administer any kind of beating, no matter how benign, unless he was focused on his sub. It took a lot of willpower to concentrate on the task at hand, rather than on her invitation. As he'd told her before, Doms were human, and right now, primal need surged through him.

At least a minute passed before he was comfortable taking a few practice swipes with the flogger.

She flinched even though he wasn't near her.

Finally satisfied, he went to her. Her body looked so beautiful, so perfect, so ready to be reddened.

He ran the handle down her spine then between her buttocks. She stayed still like a well-behaved sub. "You're ready?"

"Yes, Sir."

"I'm going to use this all over your back and buttocks, even your shoulders. I'll warn you before I increase the intensity."

"Thank you, Sir."

He used light pressure as he allowed the leather tongues to caress her naked body. She moaned with each lick, and he smelt the sharp musk of her arousal. He'd advise any Dom who claimed her to tie her up and beat her often. "Ready for more?"

"Yes, Sir."

He changed his angle and took a step back so he could get a fuller swing.

"Oh! Wow, Sir," she said. She pulled as far away from the cross as possible in silent offering.

Greedily, he accepted, flogging her bared body. Her skin turned a beautiful pink. Perspiration covered her. Her submission made her even more beautiful. "Are you doing okay, Chelsea?"

When she didn't answer, he repeated the question. She wasn't heading for subspace already, was she? He flicked his wrist with more pressure, and this time he elicited a moan from her.

"Please," she said.

"Please?"

"More. Harder. Sir."

He switched to the other flogger, and her first few moans sounded blissful. Then she fell silent. Her body went slack against the bonds. Beneath the steady rain of blows, the colour of her skin darkened from pink to light red. She made little sounds that urged him on. Realising she was mumbling, that she was flying in subspace, he tossed the flogger aside and knelt to release her ankles.

"You've pleased me immensely," he told her as stroked her skin. "I'm going to take care of you."

"Want more," she said.

"Another time. I promise." He unfastened her wrists then scooped her into his arms and carried her to his bed. She snuggled against his chest, and that alone told him she wasn't in her usual frame of mind.

Somehow he managed to pull back the duvet and place her on the mattress. He covered her and she burrowed into the pillow. "Please, Sir? Hold me?" She shivered a little.

He fought with the boots, bending over, using his hands and simultaneously trying to toe them off. All along, he had intended for her to remove them as part of her service. Seeing her charming derrière as she faced away from him and struggled had fuelled more than one fantasy.

He kicked the boots under the bed then crawled in next to her.

"Please fuck me," she said when he pulled her against him.

"Chelsea…"

She turned to face him and placed a palm against his cheek. "I want you inside me."

"You're not thinking straight. Give it a few minutes."

"I know my own mind, Sir."

He snagged her wrist. She had no idea how Goddamn difficult this was for him. "Chelsea, I'm warning you…"

She pulled her hand away and trailed it down his chest, then lower to squeeze his cock. Despite the fact he was still wearing jeans, he hardened beneath her determined touch. She tightened her grip and moved her hand up and down with a firm stroke. The vixen used her free hand to unbuckle his belt. By the time he stopped her, she'd loosened the waist and started to pull down the zipper.

"I know what I'm doing," she said. "And I want your cock."

There was only so much he could withstand. He rolled her beneath him. He pinned her arms with one hand, then somehow managed to grab a condom from the nightstand. He pressed the packet into her palm and said, "Open it."

While she did, he shucked his clothes. "Let me put it on for you?" she asked.

"I should make you use your mouth."

"If that's what Sir wishes."

His dick pulsed in response. He stood at the side of the bed, cock jutting out. Her touch wasn't skilled, and that made it all the more arousing. "Roll the condom," he said. "Don't pull it."

"Oh." Her face flushed, and that delighted him.

"Spread your legs, girl." This time he didn't hold her down, he just sank in, deep, with a single thrust. "You are ready."

"You make me insatiable, Sir."

"Pain slut."

She smiled.

He pinched her nipple. She came in a warm gush, wetting them both. He put one hand in her short locks. Because it would blur the lines, he had a rule not to kiss the women he trained. But the sight of her, her perfection, blasted away his determination. He held her and gently took her lips.

Her eyes widened, then she closed her lids.

Needing to give more, receive more, he deepened the kiss.

She responded to that like she did everything else. With passionate abandon. She met him thrust for thrust, and she shocked him by capturing the tip of his tongue between her teeth for a moment before letting go and becoming the aggressor. This was a side of her he'd never experienced, and it aroused him.

"Incredible," she murmured after he ended the kiss. She licked her upper lip. "Can I be on top, Sir?"

"Excuse me?"

"It must be the jeans, you gave me all these cowboy ideas, and I want to ride you."

He grinned and considered her idea. There was no danger in her forgetting their respective roles, so he put his hand beneath her buttocks and reversed their positions. "Straddle me then, sub. But remember, you need permission before you climax."

"After that kiss, Sir, that may not be possible."

He pinched her.

"I mean, yes, of course, Sir."

"That's what I thought you meant."

She rose onto her knees. She grasped his penis then she sank down on him. He gritted his teeth to prevent himself from coming too soon.

He held her to help guide her motions.

"Oh, yes," she said. "That's... I love the angle, Sir."

He loved the sight of her breasts jostling. She was a lovely sight and he visually feasted on her as he filled her tight cunt.

"I think I'm going to come. Sir, may I?"

He let go of her and captured her nipples. "Do it," he said, squeezing hard.

"Master Alexander!" She came, her internal muscles clamping down on him, hard.

Within a moment, he ejaculated. He pulled her tight against his chest as his balls drained. He held her for at least a minute as their breathing returned to normal.

She propped one elbow on the mattress near his head, and she feathered her fingers into his hair. "I like the way you do me, Sir. Thank you."

"We'll make a halfway decent sub out of you yet." He slapped her thigh. "You have ten minutes before we leave for dinner. Be ready, waiting near the door, dressed and kneeling."

She stayed where she was, as if she had all the time in the world, and despite the fact his now-flaccid member was sliding out of her. "There are ways to punish you if you're not ready on time," he warned. "Ways you won't enjoy."

He pushed himself up, and she scampered towards the en suite.

The red marks were already fading from her skin. It didn't appear he'd left any marks that would be visible at tomorrow night's party. That realisation didn't please him.

He decided to shower in the guest bathroom, and when he headed downstairs to grab his keys, he found her exactly where she was supposed to be, kneeling up. The ends of her hair were still damp.

"Impressive."

"I am such a very good sub, Sir."

"Stand up, lift your skirt, turn your back to me, then grab your ankles and ask me to slap you for being so saucy."

She did exactly what he said, but not in the way he intended.

She stood with the grace he demanded, despite the heels. And she flipped up the skirt, exposing her naked rear. No underwear. God save him. She performed an exquisite pivot then spread her legs so far apart that she revealed her cunt to him. She took her time and exaggerated her motions as she reached for her ankles.

"Stay there," he said.

He went into the guest powder room and grabbed a condom. Minx wanted to play with fire...? He rejoined her and teased her pussy with his fingers. "Freshly shaven?"

"Yes, Sir. You may want to replace your razor blade before using it."

So damn hot.

He slapped her cunt, hard.

She froze, then a moment later, she pushed her bottom back towards him. "Again," she demanded. "Please, Sir. Again."

She was impossible to resist. Three more times, he gave her what she begged for before dropping his trousers. Looking at her moist pussy, he vigorously fisted his cock then rolled on a condom. He gripped her hips and dragged her backwards to meet his thrust, impaling her heated sheath.

She cried out from obvious shock.

"Wow, Sir!"

He fucked her hard, holding her securely but penetrating deep, making it impossible for her to breathe.

He used her like the sub she said she was. He didn't try to pleasure her, he satisfied himself in her body.

"Oh, Sir, I want to come," she said when he spurted jism into the condom.

"You will have to wait," he said, giving a final thrust to drain the last drop. He pulled out his cock, and helped her to stand.

She faced him as she smoothed her skirt into place.

In another test, he extended the used latex. "Be a good sub and dispose of this and the wrapper."

"My pleasure, Sir."

Her response made him blink. She bent to scoop the wrapper from the floor, then she took the filled latex from him. Without a single word of protest or wrinkling her nose, she went into the small bathroom. A few moments later, he heard the sound of water running in the sink.

He had finished securing his pants when she sashayed into the room. "What are you up to?"

"I want to come, Sir. I figure behaving will help me earn it." She flashed her rear as she grabbed her purse.

"Besides, I like it when you lose control and fuck me all wild-like."

"After you." Until this trainee, he'd always been deliberate in how and where he fucked. No one goaded him. But she was getting to him. It was time to turn her over to someone else.

Chapter Eight

Tension knotted Chelsea's stomach and she picked at her dinner despite the fact the food was fabulous. He'd chosen an upscale seafood restaurant in the foothills with spectacular views of Denver and the plains in the distance. This was not the type of place she frequented. Her budget didn't stretch that far.

Even though they were dining together in a wonderful place, her mind was elsewhere. On some levels, the idea of letting someone else tell her what to do and make decisions for her had rankled. The suggestion that she should serve him in any way had annoyed her. But over the last couple of weeks, things had changed.

She recognised the myriad ways he served her, from wonderful dinners—no parsley in sight—to holding her gently, from opening doors to washing her in the shower. She'd learnt that submission wasn't a one-way street. And the more he required from her, the more he also gave. He made her feel cared for and appreciated. She had certainly not expected that when she'd approached him at the Den.

Before they'd left this evening, she'd loved the way he'd taken her from behind. His possession had been unexpected and powerful. But now her pussy throbbed from his denial.

"Not hungry?" he asked.

"Sorry. I was playing with my food, Sir." She laid her fork on top of her plate. She was looking forward to tomorrow night at the Den and finally sceneing with Master Evan C. But she was going to miss seeing Master Alexander. She realised that she was starting to care for him, deeply. Falling for a trainer was stupidity, she knew, but she hadn't seen it coming.

"Would you like to finish your wine? Or would you like to go?"

She folded her hands together in her lap. "I don't want to rush you, Sir."

He looked at her, his gaze focused on her. He frowned slightly before nodding. "I'd rather get home, as well." He signalled for the check and paid the bill.

"Thank you for dinner, Sir," she said, when he pulled back her chair.

"You have the loveliest manners," he said. "This time I want you to walk in front of me."

It seemed he gave a different order every time they were together. That was part of his plan, she supposed. With a new Dom, she wouldn't know what to expect, and so he prepared her for everything. He was good at what he did.

They waited at the valet stand, and when one of the men opened the door for her, Master Alexander said, "I'll see to the lady."

The valet nodded and accepted his tip. Master Alexander handed her into the SUV and waited while she buckled her seatbelt before closing the door.

"You seem quiet," he observed after he eased into traffic.

"Just trying to concentrate," she said, fabricated.

He shot her a sideways glance.

"I don't want to be a disappointment," she added, hoping that would dissuade him from further questions.

"You won't be." He took her hand and drew it to his lips.

The angst that had been bubbling through her since he'd denied her an orgasm became clawing desire. She needed to release the tension, and she didn't want to do it through bad behaviour. Chelsea generally felt as if she was in control of every situation, but with him, she had no idea what to do. She couldn't admit the truth, that she wanted to stay in his arms. But he also demanded she be honest with him.

"When we get back, leave your clothes inside the door and then go up to my bedroom. When I get there, I want to find you leaning over the bed, your ass cheeks spread apart."

Her mouth dried. "Yes, Sir." Obviously he intended to do more anal training this evening. She didn't object. Now that she'd become more accustomed to it, she sometimes enjoyed it. When he fucked her with the butt plug in place, the sensations made nerve endings sing. It was so tight, so overwhelming. Now that she was past the worry that the thing would be expelled when she climaxed, she anticipated those evenings.

He pulled the vehicle into the garage. She tried not to notice how normal—how wonderful—it felt to arrive home with him. She preceded him into the house. As soon as the door closed behind him, she kicked off her heels and started to unbutton her blouse.

She expected him to walk straight past her, but he paused. He dug a hand into her hair and tipped her head to one side.

He sank his teeth into the tender flesh near her shoulder. Her knees bent, and before she could lose her balance, he caught her.

"Don't keep me waiting, sub." He walked away.

Chelsea stripped where she was. Those were his instructions. She doubted he would have minded if she had undressed in the living room, but she wasn't certain. She'd learnt one thing during their time together, and that was to explicitly follow his orders. If he had commanded her to get naked in the garage, she would have done that. She had realised he looked out for her interests and never asked her to do something that would compromise her safety or modesty.

In the distance, a door closed, and she assumed he'd entered his home office. Not knowing how much time she had, she hurried upstairs to prepare for his arrival.

The beast kept her waiting.

She fought to stay focused, to harness her thoughts, to keep her ass cheeks spread. She listened intently for any sound that would indicate his imminent arrival. Just because she heard nothing, it didn't mean he wasn't standing there, watching her.

This time, he wasn't being stealthy.

She heard his footfall on the steps, then outside the door. For a moment she forgot to breathe. But he continued down the hallway. She almost relaxed, but then realised it didn't mean he wouldn't be back right away. Doing what her Dom wanted when she didn't want to or when she didn't see the point was her greatest challenge.

He kept her waiting for a few minutes before joining her.

"Perfect," he said.

Her heart raced. His approval made the wait worthwhile.

"You know I'm going to fuck your ass tonight, sub."

Her breath threatened to strangle her. She couldn't have spoken now if he paid her.

"We'll start with a small plug."

She heard the sound of his shoes. Out of her peripheral vision, she saw him place a few items on the nightstand.

He rubbed her bare buttocks. "No marks that won't fade by tomorrow," he told her.

Before she was ready, he placed the tip of the small plug against her. The silicone felt cold and wet. "Open up," he said, then he pushed it in.

She barely felt its insertion, and it took no time to accommodate to the feel.

"You're getting better at that," he told her. "Now a larger size."

She still found it a bit humiliating for him to remove a plug, but she knew protesting wouldn't change anything. In fact, he'd probably think up a diabolical way to teach her not to say anything in future.

He worked the bigger one in a little at a time, easing it in and pulling it out, then going deeper with each thrust.

She groaned when the biggest part stretched her anal ring.

"Keep your asshole exposed for me," he said. "Now you're going to take one that's larger than either of those."

"Sir..." She was tempted to move her hands.

"Your choice, sub. I can prepare you with another plug, or I can fuck you now."

Chelsea knew she should have kept her mouth shut. "Another one is fine, Sir." He eased the current one from her, and she exhaled a huge sigh of relief. The respite was short lived. Almost instantly she felt something larger demanding entrance. "Damn, Sir!"

"Relax your muscles," he coached.

She curled her toes against the unyielding floor. "I can't do this!"

He slapped her ass hard.

The distraction allowed him to sink the nasty thing in farther. "This one feels different," she said after she expelled her breath. And she hated it. It felt bruising and punishing.

"It's made from tempered glass," he said. "Unbreakable. It's considerably less forgiving than the others we've used until now."

She shuddered. Having his cock up there would feel better than this, she was sure.

He reached beneath her to play with her clit. Always this man knew how to touch her. As need built in her, he moved the glass piece around, working it in, easing it out, then pushing forward again.

She whimpered as he continued the assault on her rear. She'd never dealt with anything this horrible before.

Despite all her good intentions, she moved her hands and tried to stand. He forced her back down and he twisted the glass so that it slid in.

She panted, drenched with sweat, tears swimming in her eyes. Pain swamped her.

"Good girl."

"Fuck you," she said under her breath.

"Did you say something, sub?"

"Thank you, Sir."

He flipped her over so that she was on her back looking up at him.

"I think you were being disrespectful, girl."

She shook her head, but then she looked away and closed her eyes.

"Chelsea?"

Digging for courage, she faced him again. "You're right, Sir. I was. I'm sorry. It hurts so much, and your words struck me as condescending." She bit her lower lip, afraid of his reaction. Even in a vanilla relationship, speaking to a partner in that way was disrespectful and unacceptable. "I was out of line. I accept whatever punishment you deem necessary."

He loomed over her, fully dressed, arms folded implacably. "Do you or do you not have a safe word?"

She wanted to look away. "Yes, I do, Sir."

"Do you remember what it is?"

"Parsley, Sir."

"And do you or do you not have a way to request a pause if you can't deal with something?"

With a bravery that she wasn't feeling, she continued to meet his gaze. "Yes, Sir."

"A good sub communicates with her Master."

That wasn't what he was to her. Was it? He was a fill-in Dom. Nothing more? So why did she feel so terrible? Earlier she'd told him she hated the idea of disappointing him. He had no idea how true that was.

"Talking, expressing your feelings…that's the only way for the relationship to get deeper and richer. It develops trust. Otherwise you have something meaningless. Is that what you want?"

"No it's not, Sir." She wished he'd spank her, light up her rear, chastise her, and get it over with.

Anything other than this overwhelming sensation of shame.

"I'm going to punish you," he said.

"Yes, Sir."

"Get on all fours and fuck yourself with the plug."

She opened her mouth in shock.

"You heard me. Much harder to take than a beating, isn't it?"

"Sir... I mean..."

"Do it, girl."

"Can we negotiate this?"

"Absolutely not. Safe word and go home or do this now."

The world seemed to shift beneath her. This might be the most dreadful thing he'd ever requested of her.

"Talk to me, girl."

His use of the word was obviously intentional to reinforce their roles. "I will do what you said, but I'm embarrassed as hell. I don't want to do it. I'd rather you whip me."

"That's why I've chosen this. I've learnt a thing or two about subs during this process, and being a brat with me will only earn you time to think about your behaviour. I like flogging and belting you, but you like it, as well. Keeping that in the erotic realm is what works best with you."

She resisted the urge to cover up. She'd never felt so exposed. He didn't just see her physically, he excavated her deepest emotions.

"Anything further?"

"No, Sir."

"Then pull the plug out and reinsert it twenty times. If it needs more lube at any point, just let me know."

He continued to stand above her as she got onto all fours. She closed her eyes as she reached back and grasped the slippery glass hilt. In order to extract it, she had to curl her entire hand around the base and bear down.

She silently counted, and wished she were anyplace but here.

"Faster," he instructed.

It took all her willpower not to say something else that would get her in trouble. She'd thought she was becoming a better sub. This showed her how much further she had to go.

When she was about a dozen strokes in, he said, "Stop and give me the plug."

Quicksand. She'd give all her savings to have quicksand swallow her whole.

She watched as he squirted more of the thick lubricant on the plug. Then he gave it back to her.

"You may continue."

Wordlessly she did so, getting through the rest as quickly as possible. It became less and less difficult to put it in and pull it out, but it was every bit as uncomfortable. When she finished, she looked up at him.

"Another five," he said.

"Ah..." She stared at him in shock.

He raised his eyebrows and silently regarded her.

"Yes, Sir." Blast him. He did understand how to reinforce a message.

She took hold of the hated thing and went through the motions again. Her body was becoming fatigued from the awkward position, and her rear was starting to burn.

"That will suffice," he said.

"Thank you, Sir."

"You could have avoided those last five by remembering your manners after the first twenty."

Would she ever learn?

"Leave the plug in."

She could barely breathe with the way it filled her.

"Undress me," he said.

Chelsea was starting to regret having requested extra time with him. What the hell had she been thinking?

Moving with the plug in was difficult. Having him up there couldn't possibly be any worse than this. She untied his shoes, and he dutifully lifted each foot in turn so she could remove them. She stuffed his socks inside each. Then she undid his belt and lowered his zipper. His already-hardening cock protruded through his boxers. Watching her with the plug was clearly a turn-on for him. At least that was something.

She quickly removed his pants then she awkwardly stood — trying not to shift the plug — to unbutton his shirt. He would have thrown it aside, she knew. She laid it on the bed.

"Condom is on the nightstand."

He could have easily reached it.

"Crawl," he said.

She was ready to gnaw off the tip of her tongue.

"Now put it on me."

After she did, he added, "I recommend you lube up my dick."

Even his tone was different from earlier today. Being so disrespectful had changed something between them, and she would do anything to take it back. He was colder with her, harsher, clipping out orders. She'd told him how much she despised that. She could do anything as long as she felt connected to him. "Sir, I really am sorry," she whispered, looking up at him.

He remained implacable. His lack of response made her insides a ball of knots. Knowing she couldn't take back the last ten minutes, she pumped some lube onto him and smeared it around with her hand.

"Remove your plug and place it on the nightstand."

Imagining she was on a beach in the Bahamas drinking rum, she did as he said. Pretending to be elsewhere was the only way to survive some of these humiliations.

"Bend over the bed."

Fear made it feel as if the room temperature dropped several degrees.

"Your ass is stretched so wide," he said when she'd displayed herself, parting her ass cheeks without being told. "You look so fuckable, girl. I'm going to do you hard."

She felt his cockhead seeking entrance, and she wasn't sure she'd ever endured anything worse than this.

He took hold of her left shoulder and drove himself a little deeper, and slid his other arm beneath her midriff.

"Push out," he told her.

It hurt, but she didn't object. She wanted his flesh, rather than the cold and impersonal piece of moulded glass. She craved his possession. "Yes," she said.

He continued to ease in and pull back. Within seconds, she discovered having him inside her wasn't as bad as she imagined. It was different. A plug snuggled in, but a cock kept her spread.

"Sexy sub," he murmured.

The sound of his pleasure made her heart skip. "More, Sir."

"Are you sure you're ready?"

"I want your cock, Sir. Take me."

He held her more tightly and jerked his hips, burying himself up to his balls in her ass.

She released her hands when his thrusting forced her deeper into the mattress. She sobbed, and the sound was muffled by the bedcovers.

"Chelsea?"

"*Oh my God!* This is so good." Her reaction surprised her. She'd never felt more complete. His rigidity in her most private part filled her, awed her. Sensually, she was drowning. "I want to come, Sir."

"Do," he told her.

He lifted her upper body slightly off the mattress. That changed his angle slightly, and he penetrated even deeper. She couldn't breathe. It was as if electricity singed her skin. She rose onto her toes and arched her back. "Sir!"

"Come," he urged.

Her body trembled as the orgasm swamped her. "Never... I never experienced anything like that," she managed, her chest heaving.

"Damn, girl. I may never let you go."

"Don't." She didn't know whether she was asking him to keep her or whether she was begging him not to say that. All she knew was that nothing, other than this moment, existed for her.

He continued to fuck her hard, and a second orgasm teased her as he surged, cock thickening right before he ejaculated.

Obviously still aware of her, he moved one hand and unerringly found her clit. He stroked her, sending her over the edge one more time.

He collapsed on top of her. If this was what submission was like, about, she wanted more. This joining had not existed with anyone else.

She was barely aware of the world around her as he withdrew his spent cock and went into the bathroom.

She somehow managed to crawl up onto the bed and turn onto her side.

Moments later he pressed something warm and damp against her rear.

"Shh," he told her.

She didn't protest as he cleaned her with a washcloth. The water soothed her burning skin. A few moments later, the bed sagged beneath his weight. He eased her against him, and held her tight. She stiffened.

"I'm not open to negotiation, Chelsea. Freaking relax."

He smoothed her hair as he tucked her under his chin. Despite the fact her overnight bag was still in her car, she'd refused to spend a night with him. That spoke to an intimacy she didn't want with him. But now, here she was, in his house, his bed, his arms. And she wanted to stay. She gave herself permission to stay where she was for five minutes. That couldn't hurt anything. *Right?*

When she woke, it was the middle of the night.

She started to get out of the bed only to have him pull her tight. She knew he wasn't awake, so his grip was instinctive and domineering, but she didn't want to struggle against him and risk a confrontation.

Before she'd sorted through all of her thoughts, his warmth and strength lulled her back to sleep.

* * * *

The scent of coffee brought her to consciousness. When she opened her eyes, he was sitting on the edge of the bed, looking at her and holding two cups of coffee. She propped herself on her elbows. "Are both of those for me?"

"I was hoping you'd share."

"If I'm feeling generous," she said. She scooted to a sitting position and rested her shoulders against the headboard. She accepted a cup and inhaled deeply. "Thank you." She took a sip. He'd added the perfect splash of cream, and the beverage was hot and strong. "If you spoil me like this, I might never leave."

"What makes you think I was hoping you would?"

Their gazes locked. She looked away first. Damn. She had to stay focused on her goal. And her goal was not to play with him. It was to snare Master Evan C.

"I'd like to leave for the Den by five o'clock," he said. "Do you mind meeting here since I'm closer?"

"Perfect."

Even though he invited her to use his shower, she decided to go home. With the way her emotions were in turmoil, she needed distance and space.

As she discovered after being in her apartment for two hours, it didn't help. Being alone only made her more uncertain and restless. When she'd approached Master Alexander, this had all seemed so easy. He'd train her. She'd land Master Evan C as a client and Dom. Another success in her business and her life.

The day loomed in front of her.

After tossing in a load of laundry and straightening the house, she decided to do some work. She checked her e-mails, and she was delighted to find one from Master Evan C. Finally. He said he was interested in talking to her more about her proposal, and maybe they'd have a chance to connect at the party.

She pumped her fist in the air and swivelled her chair in circles.

But when silence echoed back mockingly, she frowned. Somehow the small victory felt hollow with no one to share it with.

There was another e-mail from her assistant. Jennifer suggested that, since Alexander Monahan hadn't responded positively to the idea of a charity fundraiser, maybe they should contact his brother.

Chelsea drummed her fingers on the keyboard. She doubted Alex would approve of her going behind his back. But if her assistant did it... Well, she knew he wouldn't like that either. But a lot of good could come from the publicity.

What the hell.

After tonight, she'd likely never see Master Alexander again. And she still had a business to run. She replied, telling Jennifer to go for it, then Chelsea decided to take a quick shower before heading to the hot tub. Luckily there were no teenage boys around, and she had the area all to herself.

Despite the fact she wanted to think about business, random images of Master Alex flashed through her mind. She saw him in jeans. Wearing dress trousers. Naked. Dragging her over his lap. Showing her a flogger. Doubling over his belt.

She'd never before had trouble with getting derailed once she had a course of action, but Master Alex consumed her.

She leaned her head back and closed her eyes. And the truth smacked her. The reason she'd hesitated in contacting his brother was that she didn't want the relationship to end. Master Alex's comment about her staying in his life stopped her pulse. He might have meant it as a joke, but part of her wanted it to be true.

So where did that leave her?

Anxiety churning in her, she opened her eyes and sat up. She needed action so that she could drown out the clamour in her head.

She showered then put some gel in her hair, squeezed the locks with her fingers. Now that it was time to dress, courage deserted her.

The idea of stripping to play with Master Evan C should have made her moist with anticipation, but it didn't. She felt such angst over the fact that she might never see Master Alex again.

She dressed in a lacy black bra, a matching thong, and some thigh-high stockings. The elastic around them kept them in place without the need for a garter belt. She added a skirt, a tight-fitting top, and a pair of ridiculously high heels.

She swiped on some mascara and applied a layer of foundation before grabbing her purse and heading for her car.

At his house, she knocked as was her custom, but he shocked her by opening the door rather than waiting for her let herself in. The sight of him made her mouth water. He wore leather pants and a T-shirt that he'd tucked into his waistband. His hair was raked back from his square forehead, emphasising his piercing brown eyes. He hadn't shaved, and that left an intentional scruffy look that made him look even more masculine. Damn.

"Shall we?" he asked.

The earth shifted beneath her stilettos. She was slightly early, but he hadn't asked her to strip. He hadn't performed an inspection. It was as if they were two acquaintances sharing a ride to the same party. After the way he'd trained her to react, his behaviour left her off-kilter.

He placed his fingers lightly at the small of her back as he led her outside to his waiting vehicle.

"You look nice," he told her as if they were going out to a simple get-together, again, as if this were just two friends hanging out. *Except for the leather pants.* The leather pants said this wasn't an ordinary date.

Until they passed through the town of Winter Park, the conversation was mainly idle chitchat. Because she couldn't take the inanity any longer, she again suggested his company hold a charity fundraiser. She neglected to mention that Jennifer was contacting his brother about it.

"Do you just try to wear people down?" he asked.

"Is it working?"

"It might, except for the fact you'd ask me to be involved," he responded, sliding her a sidelong glance.

"What if I promised you wouldn't have to do anything other than show up?"

"You wouldn't want any approval on the venue? Suggestions on the guest list?"

"Well, I would need you to—"

"There's a dental dam in my bag," he said.

"This is me shutting up," she promised.

"About tonight," he started.

"Yes?"

"I assume Evan C knows you're coming?"

"He does. He said he's looking forward to talking with me."

"I also assume you want to play with him."

Why did it feel as if she were betraying Master Alex? He seemed to be gripping the steering wheel very tightly, but that could be her imagination. "Yes." Calling him Sir seemed strange given the subtle change in their relationship since this morning. And *not* calling him Sir seemed odd.

"I'll give you the privacy you need with Evan C."

Did that also mean he was going to play with some submissives? The idea made her grit her teeth, even though she told herself her possessive feelings were ridiculous. Never in her life had she felt jealous of anyone.

All too soon, they arrived at the Den. She opted to leave her coat and purse in the vehicle. A valet opened the door for her, then Master Alexander came around and offered his hand as she negotiated the uneven terrain. High heels and the Rockies were not a good mix. "But I still think it would have made a perfect photo op," she said.

He ignored her.

Once they were inside, he said, "Please stay a bit behind me. Speak only when spoken to. Address men as Sir and women as Ma'am."

"Yes, Sir." Having him give her instructions made this a bit more comfortable.

Master Damien greeted them and invited them to grab a drink from the bar downstairs, and he asked her if she recalled the Den's safe word.

"Halt, Sir."

He nodded. "Enjoy your time with us, Ms Barton."

"Thank you, Sir."

"Much better behaved than last time," he observed to Master Alexander.

She didn't wince, and that alone showed her how far she'd come from her previous visit.

"Something to drink?" Master Alexander offered when Master Damien excused himself.

"Please, Sir," she said. "Wine, maybe. Merlot. Cabernet. I'm really not picky."

She followed him down the stairs. While he fetched them each a drink, she kept a lookout for Master Evan C.

She saw him in the corner, chatting with a sub who was wearing a purple wristband, indicating she'd been hired by the Den.

He looked so different from any other Dom here. Most were in black. He wore white. A bright red scarf was wrapped around his neck. He belonged on stage, rather than at a BDSM party.

Master Alexander returned with her wine and a bottle of water for himself.

"You'll do fine," he told her, raising his bottle in a salute to her. "You've learnt a lot. You should be proud of yourself."

"I'm nervous as hell, Sir." She sipped from her glass.

"Why?"

"Probably just the idea of playing with someone new."

"It's a good experience. Concentrate on pleasing your Dom. No matter who he is."

When Master Evan C's submissive left, Chelsea squared her shoulders.

"Go on, girl," Master Alexander said.

On impulse she kissed his cheek. "Thank you for everything."

He grinned, but he didn't look happy. "I'll be here when you get back."

She moved away, and she looked over her shoulder, to make sure he meant it.

Master Evan C frowned a bit, evidently forgetting they'd agreed to meet. "Chelsea Barton," she said, offering her hand.

"The PR chick. You've finally had some training?"

"I have."

"Your manners suck."

"I beg your pardon?"

"You don't know how to address a Dom?"

That stung. "Of course, I do, Sir."

"You want to go to a private room?"

Her heart leapt. This was the moment she'd been waiting for. "I'd like that, Sir."

"Down the hall."

Like a good sub, she followed him. Out of the corner of her eye, she caught sight of Master Alexander. He was watching her. Damn, he was handsome. Guilt stabbed her as she gave a quick wave.

"Are you with me or with him?" Master Evan C asked.

"With you, Sir. Of course." She followed Master Evan C down the hallway. The walk reminded her of the first night with Master Alexander. The same set of nerves that had assailed her then gnawed her stomach now.

"Get your clothes off and get your ass on the cross."

"Uhm…are we going to talk about a safe word?"

"You one of them pussy girls? I thought you wanted to do business with me."

She looked at him. His blue eyes were wide, unblinking, calculating.

"I'm not into being abused, Sir, not for anything or anyone."

"Heard talk about you last time, that you scream so much you need a gag."

She shuddered.

"Get your clothes off, bitch."

Chelsea debated what to do. Master Alex had called her a slut during a scene, but the tone, the inflection had been different. It had been sexy and it turned her on. This was insulting. Before she could speak again, he grabbed her shirt, tugged it over her head and brutally squeezed her right breast.

She could barely breathe. The grip didn't arouse her. She grabbed him around the wrist and said, "Sir, that hurts."

"What? Your tit's delicate?" He laughed. "Of course it hurts."

"Please." She dug her fingernails into his skin. "Halt."

"What the fuck? I thought you'd been getting some training."

"Yeah. I have. Enough to know that I don't want a Dom like you. Let go of me."

"You've been fucking stalking me, begging for this."

She shook her head. "You're making a mistake. I think you have talent. But I thought you were a different kind of Dom." She blinked back the tears stinging her eyes, determined, damned determined, not to let the bastard see he was hurting her. "I said halt and I mean it."

"You're serious?"

"Deadly."

He blinked. "Cock tease."

She refused to allow his words to goad her. What Master Alexander had said all along was true. Submission was a gift you gave, not something that could be demanded. There was a big difference between submission and a little kink, and an even greater distinction between submission and masochism. Master Evan C was more a sadist than anything, she assumed. And she had no interest in that. She dug her fingernails into his skin. "Take your hand off me immediately."

When he didn't let her go, she had another realisation. She'd allowed her career hunger to drive feelings in her personal life. You're The Star would benefit from having Evan C on their client list. She'd fallen in love with the idea of a partnership with him. Her ambition had blinded her. "Last chance before I shout out the house safe word," she said. "Take your Goddamn hand off me."

He released her. The pain of the blood rushing back into her breast stole her next breath. "You know, Evan C, you have some natural talent. You'll do well if you don't allow your bad behaviour to fuck it up."

"You giving me career advice?"

"I won't send a bill."

"You're a tough chick."

"I'll take that as a compliment." She snatched her shirt from the floor and pulled it over her head, pretending her world hadn't changed in the last ten minutes. Everything she'd thought she wanted, hungered for, focused on, no longer mattered.

He wrapped his scarf around his neck. "I'll find someone a bit more accommodating. Someone who isn't fickle." He strode from the room.

She took a moment to stop shaking before following him from the room.

As she neared Master Alexander, she overheard Master Evan C say, "You did a shitty job of training her."

She kept her head high, as if she were wearing a posture collar. She'd done nothing wrong, and she wasn't in the least ashamed.

"If she chose not to scene with you, I think I did an excellent job of teaching her about the important things."

Chelsea almost cheered. Master Alexander — her hero.

Master Evan C walked, or rather stalked, to the bar and Brandy, whose face lit up when she saw him.

Master Alexander draped an arm around her shoulder and pulled her closer. "What the hell happened?"

"I figured out I want nothing to do with him." She smiled. "If it's all right with you, Sir, I would like to go home."

He nodded. Purposefully, he moved her towards the stairs, thanked Master Damien for his hospitality, then headed for the front door where he instructed the valet to bring the car around.

How could she have ever protested being treated like this? It was more like being a princess than a submissive. She wished every man behaved so courteously.

He reached across her to fasten her safety belt, then locked and closed her door. She stared unseeingly at the darkened landscape, her emotions in turmoil. She'd got what she wanted, or what she had thought she wanted. And so, now what? How did she go back to her regular life? And the idea of finding her perfect man was even more impossible than it had ever been. Where would she find someone worthy of her submission, and did she even want to give it?

She needed time alone. Lots of it.

Master Alexander waited until they had summited Berthoud Pass before looking at her. "Do you want to talk about it?"

"There's nothing really to say. He has a different opinion of submission than I do." She looked over at the man who had taught her so much. Since it was dark, his face was in shadows. That didn't matter, though. She knew every plane and angle intimately.

"Are you hurt?"

She straightened her shoulders. "Not at all." In fact she had more strength and courage than she'd ever had, gifts she'd received from her two-week journey into submission. "I've never been better, Sir."

He took his gaze from the road long enough to cast a quick glance in her direction. "Seriously?"

"I owe you a lot, Sir. I wouldn't have handled Master Evan C as well as I did without everything I've learnt from you." She reached over to trace her fingertips down his arm. "Thank you."

"It's been my pleasure," he said. "I've enjoyed training you. And the fact you stood up for yourself makes me proud." For a moment, he closed his hand around hers. When he pulled it away, she put on her brave face and pretended her heart wasn't breaking. Facing down Evan C had been easy for one reason.

She was in love with Master Alexander.

Chapter Nine

"Are you out of your mind?" Alex sat back in his chair, steepled his fingers, and looked at his younger brother. Goddamn it. He knew how persistent Chelsea was. Why hadn't it occurred to him that she'd take a backdoor approach? Gavin was younger, more idealistic, more outgoing than Alex. The conniving vixen had gone behind his back, and now he was involved in an epic battle with his only sibling. He set his jaw. She needed to be turned over his lap and paddled hard. "A charity fundraiser is the last thing we need to be involved in."

"I think she's right. We need to get more involved in the community."

"We make plenty of contributions."

"Plenty that no one knows about," Gavin countered.

Though they'd lost a number of clients when their sterling reputation had been tarnished, many, like Damien, had stayed. Doing something to restore some of the lustre might not be a bad idea, but Christ, there had to be something different.

"Our PR firm did a good job of damage control," Gavin continued. "They just haven't done shit since then. You can show up or not. I signed a contract with Jennifer yesterday."

"Jennifer? Don't you mean Chelsea?"

Gavin shook his head. "She's an administrative assistant with You're The Star."

Chelsea really knew how to work a potential client. She'd refused to listen when he said no. Instead, she'd tried another approach. Clever girl.

Alex listened to his brother extol the virtues of the PR plan, including press releases and a social media campaign. But he realised one thing. It was a good idea. He still wanted to tan her hide, and he planned to do just that. And the fact she'd continued to try to land his business even though they hadn't seen each other for a few weeks meant... What? Nothing? That she still wanted to work together? Was he just business to her? They'd had an arrangement for him to train her, and she'd done an excellent job.

He shouldn't have been surprised that she hadn't contacted him after the night at the Den, but he was. Half a dozen times he'd picked up the phone, but each time, he'd pushed the end icon before the call connected. He told himself she had only asked him to teach her about submission so that she could capture Master Evan C's attention.

But when that hadn't worked out, she'd probably returned to dating vanilla men. Over the years, he'd been involved with a lot of women, from sceneing, to training, to dating. They'd all had one thing in common. Submission had been natural to them. For Chelsea, it hadn't been. He'd watched her struggle with the mental implications. She'd done well. She'd been a good, if not excellent, student. But there was no doubting the fact it didn't come easily.

As he'd tried to teach her, kink—a little spanking, maybe some blindfolds and gags—was different from a BDSM lifestyle. Plenty of people brought a little spice into their bedrooms. If that was what she wanted, so be it.

That wouldn't satisfy his desires, however.

He enjoyed the protocol associated with D/s. He liked to care for his woman, but he had expectations in return. He had no issue with them having a high-profile career. But only one person could be in charge in a relationship.

Gavin snapped his fingers. "Earth to Alex?"

"Yeah." He leant forwards, over his desk. "Sorry."

"I was saying that all you need to do is show up and do the meet-and-greet. I'll handle the planning on this end. Fucking stop scowling, will you?"

He listened to Gavin ramble for a few more minutes. His younger brother had already set a date—after checking the corporate calendar—and agreed to the venue, which You're The Star had secured at no charge in exchange for tons of promotion. His Chelsea Barton was a savvy businesswoman.

His.

That thought stunned him.

He'd taken her to the Den because he'd agreed to, not because he'd wanted to. Watching her and Evan C head down the hallway to a private room had sent a surge of hot blood through his veins.

He'd grabbed a beer from the bar and spent a few minutes talking with Gregorio. He'd said that the Den often fielded requests for trainers and wondered if Alex was back in the business. He'd said he wasn't. Chelsea was enough for him.

"Have you heard a word I've said?"

"I stopped listening five minutes ago."

Gavin stood. "Don't be an ass about this, got it?" Without another word, he left Alex's office. Gavin slammed the door to punctuate his point.

Alex picked up the phone and selected Chelsea's name from his list of contacts.

Not surprisingly, he reached her voicemail. He followed with a text message, giving her five minutes to respond.

At four minutes and fifty seconds, she called. "It's Chelsea," she said, her voice quiet, and quivery, as if with emotion.

He knew he could be making that up. She might be in the middle of something, maybe a meeting, perhaps afternoon traffic. But she'd called him back in less than the allotted time. He told himself that meant something. Or at least he fucking hoped it did. "You won."

"No," she countered. "Monahan Capital did. The kids who will benefit also won."

"You went behind my back."

"I did the right thing," she countered.

Always the fighter. "You have a lot to answer for." He pictured her kneeling up, awaiting his punishment.

"And who's going to hold me accountable?"

Silence hung between them, thick, palpable, laden. Had she issued a challenge? Or was it a rhetorical question? He was generally a man of action, and trying to figure out what she meant gnawed at him. He didn't want to misstep, but he'd phoned her with the intention of seeing her again.

But to what end?

He only wanted to be involved with a woman who wouldn't fight him on every issue. He needed a sub. He wanted her. Alex didn't consider himself a fool, but he sure as hell was behaving like one. "Dinner?" he asked.

She was silent for so long that he thought she wasn't going to answer. When she spoke, her voice was more subdued than he'd ever heard it. "I don't think that's a good idea. But thank you for the offer," she said before ending the call.

He sat back and reached for a pencil. He drummed it against the desktop.

She might have turned him down, but that didn't mean anything. Like a good girl, she'd called him straight back. She'd hesitated for a long time before refusing his invitation. He was more comfortable with facts and figures than with relationships, but unless he missed his bet, she'd wanted to agree.

He wasn't sure where that knowledge left him or what to do with it. For the first time in his life, a woman had perplexed him.

* * * *

Chelsea held her clipboard close to her chest and looked around the large room one last time.

She, Jennifer and their team had spent six intense weeks doing the preparation work, and the big day had finally arrived.

In keeping with the hoedown theme, red-and-white chequered cloths covered rectangular tables. Bright yellow sunflowers dropped their fat faces over skinny vases.

Two bars were being stocked with good beer and fine wine. A popular band was tuning up on the stage, and Jennifer was in last-minute discussions with the lead singer about the timing of announcements. Tables filled with silent auction items lined the walls. And the scent of the barbecue beef and pork wafted over the mountain valley.

For a month, they'd sent press releases to all the Denver outlets and to the news media in all the nearby towns, and they'd spent a day in the area about two weeks ago talking to local merchants, and pinning up flyers.

She had updated Monahan Capital's Web site with information, she'd done several e-mail campaigns to everyone they'd ever done business with, and she'd shamelessly peppered every social networking site and asked her friends and family to do the same. She'd blasted the band's fans, the catering company's client list, the charity's donors, even the lodge's employees and past guests. For good measure, she'd contacted some celebrity spokespeople, too.

She'd pretty much notified everyone in North America of the event.

The weather had even cooperated, so they could also utilise the outdoor space. If things went as well as she and Jennifer hoped, they would need all the room they could get.

She checked her watch. Thirty minutes until the doors opened. Things were ahead of schedule, thank God. A table, manned by several temporary workers, was in the foyer. They'd been trained to sell raffle tickets as well as encourage high bidding on the auction items.

Everyone was even dressed according to her specifications. She and Jenn each wore denim skirts, white blouses, and they'd added a red bandana around their necks as an accessory.

She'd tried to think through everything. Truthfully, her company had never worked harder on an event. This could put her firm on the map, but there was much, much more than that on the line.

She wanted to please Master Alexander. He'd made it clear, even to Jenn, that he wanted nothing to do with the fundraiser. He didn't like being thwarted by anyone, especially his younger brother.

Chelsea told herself the event mattered only to her portfolio. But that was a lie. She still wanted to please him. It was the same reason she'd practised for so many hours while he'd been training her. His good opinion of her mattered. Maybe too much.

When he'd invited her to dinner over a month ago, she'd desperately wanted to accept. But for her own sanity, she'd refused. She loved him too much to hang out, or even scene. Every evening when she finally slowed down, she thought of him. Keeping memories of their time together at bay had become a full-time, and mostly futile, job.

Chelsea had mentally rehearsed how she was going act when they came face-to-face. She'd be wearing a bright smile. She would exude tons of confidence as she offered her hand and wished him lots of success. Her demeanour would be professional, and she'd give a quick excuse and move off and see to some pressing demand. At the end of the evening, she'd leave Jennifer to deal with the Monahan brothers while she wrapped up the other details. The two of them would drive home together in Jennifer's car. Chelsea had thought everything through.

"Haven't we talked about your posture?"

The sound of Master Alexander's voice snaked up her spine and she froze, fear all but holding her immobilised. How the hell had she missed his arrival?

"Face me, please."

It took several seconds to regain control of her faculties. What stunned her most was her instinctive reaction. The sound of his voice made her bend her knees before she caught herself. And it never occurred to her to refuse to do as he asked.

As she turned, she straightened her shoulders and pasted on the smile she'd tried out in front of the mirror this morning. Oh, God. How was it possible that he was even more handsome than she remembered? His dark hair was styled back from his forehead, exposing its firm angularity. He wore tight-fitting blue jeans, cowboy boots, and a denim shirt. He'd skipped a tie and, instead, had left the top button of his shirt undone.

Her clipboard still against her chest, she offered her right hand to him. All of a sudden she wished she'd worn sexy, rather than comfortable shoes. "Nice to see you, Alex."

"Master Alexander," he corrected. "Or Sir will do."

She wasn't tempted to look around to see if anyone was watching. But she didn't respond in kind. "I hope the party is everything you deserve."

"It's going to be wonderful." He glanced at her hand, but he didn't take it.

No one had ever done that before, so she wasn't sure what to do next. Drop it? Wait? This man, more than any other, made her feel awkward.

"I've received daily updates on your progress and God knows I think you contacted every person I've ever known. I've heard from friends I had in kindergarten."

She dropped her hand, and because she wasn't sure what to do, gripped the clipboard tighter. "Hopefully we've contacted hundreds more you've never heard of."

"You've done well," he told her. "And you're going to get what you deserve."

"Ah…"

"I think we could start with a spanking for your lack of respect."

Her mouth dried. This was exactly why she had refused to go out with him. Responding to him was all too easy. More than anything she wanted to feel his hand on her bare buttocks.

"And then we will move on to the fact you went behind my back."

She searched his features. His tone was neutral, and one brow was cocked, but more questioningly than anything. He didn't appear angry.

"And when you're ready to tell us both the truth, we'll go on from there."

"The truth?" She scowled. "I have no idea what you're talking about."

"It hit me about a week ago. I know a lot about you. You're not a coward. When I invited you to dinner, you should have accepted, if for no other reason than to have another opportunity to hammer me about this event and ensure my cooperation."

Her breaths were becoming shorter and closer together.

"But you turned me down," he continued. "So I started to wonder what you were afraid of."

He took a step towards her, but she stood her ground, and that was one of the more difficult things she'd ever done.

"I wanted to know if you were more scared of me or yourself."

"You don't frighten me, Alex," she lied.

"No?"

This time, when he entered her comfort zone, she took a step back. A man with a camera and a badge walked into the room. Jennifer caught her eye and indicated she would handle the reporter. Chelsea gave the other woman a quick nod.

"I saw the way you reacted to the sound of my voice. You wanted to kneel."

"No." She shook her head.

"Another three spanks for every lie you tell yourself, sub."

"I..."

"Admit it."

She was pissed off at herself for backing up, so this time, she moved towards him, juggling the clipboard to one side as if it were armour. With her free hand, she pointed a finger at him. "You want the truth? Fine. I'll give it to you straight up. But brace for impact. I have something to tell you and when I do, you're going to run so fast an Olympian couldn't catch you."

"Try me."

Damn him. Did he always have to be so confident? She was shaking with fury, with embarrassment, and her jaw ached from grinding her teeth. She glanced around to ensure everything was under control before continuing with her same quiet anger, "I'm not just a sub."

"Fine."

"Fine?"

"I'm listening."

"I'm a woman."

He swept his gaze down her body. "A very beautiful one who is wearing far too many clothes."

"Would you be serious?"

"I am. Deadly." He took hold of her shoulders.

His touch, the scent of him, the power of him made her dizzy. "I will not be a play toy. I've realised I no longer fight against the idea of submission. You were right initially. I did think BDSM was about feathers and playful swats on the ass, maybe a few scarves for bondage. But submission is a certain mindset. It's about caring enough about a person that his needs become paramount. Pleasing him pleases me."

His grip tightened painfully, and she winced.

"Have you been playing with anyone else?" he demanded.

"Oh for fuck's sake." She exhaled. Why had he chosen now for a confrontation? Then she reminded herself she'd been too chicken to meet with him when he'd asked. She should have been prepared for this. "It's none of your business, but for the record, no. I haven't been with anyone else. I can tell you this, I will not give my submission without a great deal of thought. I do like kink. As you suggested, it's different from subjugating your own will. My submission needs to be earned by the right man. And the right man is someone I love." She set her chin. "And someone who loves me in return."

"Is that all?"

She tried to pull away, and he only tightened his grip. She'd all but confessed her love and he responded with that?

"You're not the only stubborn one," he confessed. "I told myself I didn't want another submissive after Liz. But I learnt a thing or two, especially after I saw you with Evan C. Liz would have surrendered to him, no matter how brutal he was, and she would have enjoyed it. Seeing you at the Den, your strength, resolution, determination, it all taught me something. You stood up for yourself."

His grip turned more reassuring. And it was everything she could do not to lean into it, into him.

"Of course you should only offer your submission to a man you love, and a man who loves you in return."

"What are you saying?" she asked, searching his face.

The noise level increased as guests started to arrive.

"We'll continue this conversation later."

Damn. Double damn. How was she supposed to get through the next few hours?

As if reading her mind, he said, "You've tortured me for six weeks, Chelsea. You can wait another few hours to see me mastered."

"I—"

"Chelsea, the mayor of the town is here," Jennifer said, with a quick smile at both of them as an apology. "Can I have Alex for a quick photo op?"

"You're mine, Chelsea," he said, before releasing her.

She watched him walk away, and she clutched the clipboard close as if it were a lifeline on a storm-tossed sea.

Then she couldn't think at all.

She'd planned it so that alcohol would flow before dinner, encouraging people to bid higher on the silent auction items. So far, her strategy seemed to be working.

Master Damien showed up, with Gregorio at his side. As always, the Den's owner looked dapper and debonair as he sipped a glass of wine, while Gregorio drank from a mug of draught beer and surveyed the room while conveying the idea he was someone you didn't want to meet in a dark alley. Jenn looked at Gregorio and gave a thumbs-up before turning to answer a question.

"Everything is all set at the Den for the private escape for you and Master Alex," Master Damien said after she greeted them.

She blinked. She wasn't sure she'd heard him above the band's din. "It is? I mean, it is, Sir?"

"Oh."

Gregorio grinned, but nothing about it softened his features. In fact, he just looked more ferocious. His earring glittered in the light. "Good thing you're wearing boots with the way you just stepped in it, boss."

Master Damien sipped from his wine. "Well, yes, perhaps you two should have a private discussion."

"I think I will, Sir."

"Drink up, boss."

She excused herself, but she was waylaid with a half dozen questions. More guests than their wildest estimates had suggested arrived, and so there were decisions needed about extra food and more beverages.

These were her favourite kinds of problems.

She started negotiating with the catering company, and the band's lead singer interrupted the festivities to say that one of Monahan Capital's owners had an announcement. Across the room, she looked at Jenn. The younger woman shrugged as if to say this surprised her, as well.

Alex took the stage, commanded it, really.

He thanked everyone for coming, commended You're The Star on their excellent work, then he called up a girl who'd been helped by the children's charity the evening was benefiting. He crouched next to the beautiful child, who had long dark hair and big, luminous brown eyes.

Chelsea wasn't sure she would have had the courage to call the girl on stage, but Alex did, and it had clearly been prearranged. He placed his arm around her shoulder as he held the microphone for her.

She spoke in a halting tone, telling her story and expressing her gratitude. She was as articulate as she was gorgeous. And people's eyes began to fill with tears. As she ended, Chelsea applauded, and she knew the evening would be a huge success, due in part to Alex's brilliance.

The band struck up a ballad, and Alex found her.

Words weren't needed, and none were said, as he led her outside, wrapped her in his arms, and held her as they danced.

"Alex..."

"Master Alexander."

"Master Alexander—"

"Later," he interrupted.

He feathered his hands into her hair and drew her against him. She went without protest, laying her head on his chest. For a moment, she wanted to pretend everything was perfect.

An apologetic Jenn interrupted as the last notes faded.

"We need to start announcing the winners of the silent auction."

She checked her watch. Jenn was a master time manager. A silent auction was a delicate thing. It was critical to collect funds before people left, and they needed a process to claim their prizes. And sometimes, help was needed to carry out the bigger items.

"Go," Master Alexander told her when she started to make her apologies.

Master Alexander.

Realising she thought of him that way changed something inside her. Alex was a business associate. Master Alexander was a Dom. *Her* Dom.

She was aware of both Monahan brothers assisting with various aspects of the evening, congratulating attendees on their winning bid, thanking people for coming, encouraging donations in the numerous fishbowls.

At the end of an evening like this, adrenaline generally receded and dropped her on her ass with exhaustion. She would often sleep for twelve hours. But today all she could think about was him.

Rather than being tired, she seemed to gain energy. It was as if the pent-up hurt of the past six weeks had gathered enough steam to push her to the top of a fourteen-thousand-foot summit.

When the caterers had packed up, easier than usual since there were no leftovers, and the band had loaded their instruments, the landlords showed up to lock the building. After the last goodbyes had been said, Alex appeared by her side. "Jennifer said you rode with her."

She nodded.

"I made your excuses. You'll be going home with me."

"I..."

"Your mouth looks attractive when it's gaping open like that. Makes me want to put a gag in it."

She shut her mouth.

"I've always particularly enjoyed your intelligence," he said. He took hold of her elbow and guided her towards the door. "Say goodnight to Gavin and Jennifer," he instructed her. But he gave her no time to say a word.

Jennifer smiled. Gavin gawked.

"You two concocted this," Master Alexander said. "You two can finalise the details."

He paused long enough for her to gather her belongings from the kitchen and then led her to the parking lot. His car seemed to be parked half a mile away, and the midnight Rocky Mountain air nipped at her exposed skin.

As always, he saw that she was in safely and buckled tight before sliding into the driver's seat.

How predictable was that?

He always intended to be in the driver's seat, literally and figuratively.

Master Alexander flipped a switch to turn on her seat heater. She did like some of the luxuries he took for granted.

The drive home was filled with discussion about the event. He'd yet to admit it had been a great idea, but he commented on all the things that had gone right.

He ignored her when she gave him her address and instead, he turned into his familiar neighbourhood. "You need to get accustomed to it," he said.

"What? You bossing me around?" she said, turning to face him as he parked the car in the garage.

"That. And living here."

She started to protest, but he opened the vehicle door.

"Didn't you hear me earlier?" she asked when they were inside his house. She'd followed him into the kitchen, and her nerves were stretched like a high wire.

The silence echoed around them. He folded his arms as he towered over her.

Boldly, she pressed on. This was too important to ignore. "I won't give my submission to a man unless I love him and he loves me in return. The rest is just BDSM games."

"I heard you," he said quietly. "Present yourself to me, *sub*."

She heard the intentional inflection on the term.

"Now."

With the last word, there was a subtle change in his voice. Commanding undercurrents laced his tone. His words had been neither a game nor a request.

Her fingers shaking, she stripped. As she folded her clothes, she wondered if this could mean what she hoped it did.

She could hardly think, and had to trust her memory to help her perform the right actions. There was something soothing and comfortable about being here, with him, in this circumstance. Homecoming.

He inspected her, but more gently than he ever had before, cupping her breasts and squeezing with the most arousing of touches. He tweaked her nipples and pulled on them.

She moaned. Even her fantasies as she'd masturbated hadn't compared to this.

"Smooth and silky," he observed, looking at her mound. "And did you also do an excellent job of shaving your labia?" Rather than waiting for an answer, he ran his fingers up the inside of her pussy lips. He continued to rub her clit.

She jerked in helpless response.

"One might think you were hoping this happened tonight," he said.

Since that was the absolute truth, she saw no point in lying. "I was," she confessed.

He rubbed her clit harder, then he inserted a finger inside her. "You're perfect for me, Chelsea."

Before she could respond, he resumed his Dom mode and dropped his hand, leaving her frustratingly on the edge. "Crawl into the living room like a good pet. Kneel up near the fireplace, and wait for me there."

He remained where he was, implacable and Dominant as she lowered herself to the cold tile floor and crawled past him. She realised she didn't find this at all humiliating. Somehow she'd moved past that to the point that she responded because he said so, and because she wanted to follow his instructions.

She only had to wait a few minutes until he joined her. Two lengths of rope dangled from his hands. "In keeping with the evening's theme, I'm going to use rope to bind you while I give you the thrashing you've earned."

Her pussy moistened at his brutal words.

From his back pocket, he pulled the bandana she'd had around her neck. "This," he said, "will serve as a much-needed gag. Open up."

With a scowl, she did so.

He wadded the cotton kerchief and shoved it in her mouth

"Spit it out and deal with my wrath."

She shook her head.

"Smart girl. We'll use a safe signal for the next few minutes," he told her. "Keep in mind you'll be over my knee getting your hide tanned. Your hands and feet will both be bound. Give me your wrists."

She extended her hands. God, he looked so intimidating in his jeans and boots, like a Western lawman out to bring in a criminal whose picture was on a wanted sign.

"Now stand," he told her.

He had to know how difficult that was for her, with her hands all but useless. Somehow she managed it, not at all gracefully.

He bent to tie her ankles. The rope abraded her skin, adding a whole new sensation. Wryly she thought they should have had a satin and lace theme for the evening.

With great intent, he pulled off his belt. "Cowhide for your skin," he said. He doubled over the leather and snapped it together in front of her face. Then he snared her chin with his thumb and forefinger. "I'm going to punish you, Chelsea. But it's more than that. You're going to be beaten until you can admit the truth to both of us. This will hurt."

The bandana made it impossible to swallow properly, so she nodded.

"Do you accept my punishment?"

She sought reassurance in the depths of his rich brown eyes. Again she nodded.

"Do you freely give your submission?"

Nothing had ever mattered more to her than this moment. He knew what he was asking from her, and also what he was offering. A third time, she gave her assent.

With strong and perfunctory movements, he scooped her up, sat on the couch, then deposited her across his lap. She desperately wriggled around, trying to find a position that wouldn't end with her being dumped on the hardwood flooring.

Beneath her, she felt the scratch of denim and the pure power of his legs. This would no doubt hurt, as he'd promised. But she craved it.

"Show me a safe signal."

As best as she could, she rolled onto her right side.

"Not what I expected," he said. "But it will work." He spoke as he rubbed her skin. "You will feel eight of the hardest hits you've ever experienced. You will take them."

She shuddered.

"You can think whatever you want," he continued. "I don't care if you cry enough to fill a horse trough, in fact, I might like that. You've made me suffer, sub, and you will pay."

She wanted to see his face. They'd talked about that, so she knew his behaviour was intentional. And she had to trust him. He'd never asked for it. But he'd earned it.

He increased the speed of his rubs, until her breasts jiggled.

"Are you ready?"

She wanted it over bad enough that she nodded. The first hit across both buttocks made her go rigid. The pain startled and seared.

"That was just the beginning."

Tears welled in her eyes. There was no way she could take eight like that.

The bastard landed the next two almost directly on top of the first one. She kicked. She silently wailed.

"Not even halfway," he told her.

His words were shocking. He wasn't being encouraging. Rather, he seemed a bit discouraging, as if this were a test.

Fuck him.

She could take his punishment, submit to him, love him. He'd broken her. She'd given him the truth. All of it.

Intentionally, she exhaled and relaxed her muscles.

He blazed another three across the backs of her legs. Tears welled and fell, racing down her cheeks. She never even considered using her safe signal.

She willed him to give her the next two in the same rapid succession he'd delivered the last few.

He waited. And waited. Time became an interminable enemy.

She closed her eyes, let her body go limp, and waited.

He finished her off with a blaze of glory that left her sobbing behind the bandana. He tossed the belt away and the metal buckle clattered as it hit the floor.

At one time, after receiving a beating like that, she might have told him to fuck off. Tonight, when he flipped her over and extracted the fabric from her mouth, she looked up at him. She saw conflicting emotion in his face, pain and comfort. He hurt as much as she did. Simply, past the knot of emotion in her throat, she said, "I love you."

Tears glazed the eyes of her big, bad Dom. And so, she saw, the Master became the mastered.

He manoeuvred her so that she was lying on the couch. He worked the bonds free, and she noticed that his fingers shook.

Finally, he helped her to sit, then he took hold of her forearms and pulled her to a standing position so he could cradle her. "I have loved you for a long time, Chelsea. Enough to let you go with another man if that was what you really wanted."

"I don't want anyone else." Now that the tears had started, she couldn't stop them. "I love you. You, Sir."

"If there's to be any kind of relationship between us, we need honesty. That was part of the reason for the strapping. I wanted to break you of the need to hide."

"I got the message," she said. Her buttocks burned from his fury. "I promise."

"And I promise to never hold back on you. If you had come to me at any point, Chelsea, you wouldn't have felt my wrath as you did tonight."

"I understand, Sir."

"I love you, Chelsea." He tugged back on her head so that she had to look at him. "Be mine. My submissive. My slut. My wife."

"Yes. Be my husband, my love, my Dominant. But please, first, fuck me. Claim me, Sir. Please."

"My pleasure."

Over the past six weeks, she had ached for him. Somewhere at the back of her mind, she'd known there was no one else for her. Jenn had tried to fix her up. Sara, who'd originally taken her to the Den and warned her to be careful with Master Alex, had even given Chelsea's number to another Dom. But she'd had no interest in any of them.

He carried her upstairs. Keeping her balanced, he pulled back the bedcovers, then laid her on the mattress. He undressed, tossing his clothes haphazardly around the room, before ripping open a condom, and rolling the sheath down his cock.

"Later I want you from behind. Now, I just want to look at your face as you tell me again that you'll marry me."

He bent over her and licked her cunt, eating her out until she was tossing her head deliriously.

"Tell me," he urged.

She heard the threat. There would be no orgasm until she said the words. "Yes, yes, yes, a hundred times yes. I'll marry you."

He looked up. "Soon."

"If you say so, Sir."

"I've reserved the Den. Damien can marry us, and we can stay and honeymoon there for a few days."

"Planning ahead, Sir?"

He knelt between her legs, cockhead pressing against her cunt. "Chelsea, at some point you'll understand. You're mine."

He drove into her with a single, hard, fast stroke.

"I'd do anything, take as long as needed, keep you hogtied, but I wasn't going to let you go."

She lifted her legs and wrapped them around his waist.

"You know," he said. "You're not always a naughty sub."

"No?"

"Sometimes you're very naughty."

"It sounds as if you might need to train that out of me, Sir?"

"Every day, if necessary," he said, reaching between them to press his thumb against her clit.

He kept her gaze ensnared. She loved watching him watch her.

With a raised eyebrow, he increased the force of his thrusts, pistoning his hips as he fucked her hard. Then he pressed harder on her sensitive nub.

She arched and screamed out her orgasm.

Only when she was satisfied did he come.

He collapsed on top of her, somehow also managing to hold her tight. "I love you, Chelsea."

"And I love you, Sir." She exhaled as much as she could with such a large man bearing down possessively on her.

"I need to get some arnica on your stripes."

"I'm okay if they stay red for a while," she confessed. Seeing them in the mirror for a few days would be a delicious reminder of the evening together.

He lifted onto one shoulder. "I want you healed so I can tawse you in a few days."

She ran her fingers through his combed-back hair.

"But first..." he began.

"Yes?"

"To continue your hoedown theme, you get to be a cowgirl and ride me."

"I thought men weren't good for a second time so quickly."

"Girl, it's going to be a while before I've had enough of you."

She giggled as he moved quickly, rolling them over. He made short work of disposing of the condom in the trash and donning another. She straddled him, taking his cock deep.

"Sit up straight. Show me those beautiful titties."

She drew her shoulder blades together.

"That's it."

He grabbed her breasts, then pinched and twisted her nipples viciously. She orgasmed on a loud scream. "Master!"

"That's it," he said. "That's what I wanted to hear." He took her head between his palms and pulled her down until her face was within inches of his. "My sub," he said.

"Yours, Sir."

He kissed her passionately, sealing the deal.

MASTERED
Sierra Cartwright

He can't say he
wasn't warned...

OVER THE
LINE

Mastered: Over the Line

Sierra Cartwright

Released July 2013

Excerpt

Chapter One

Michael Dayton caught a whiff of spiced vanilla, and he turned his head to find the source.

The view of the woman passing by walloped him. He only managed a brief look at her face, not enough to make out her eye colour, but on a primal level he noted the softness of her mouth and the sexy red colour that accented her lips.

She kept moving in the direction of the fire pit. And like the male he was, he didn't look away. How could he? She was tiny, compact, with blonde hair tumbling over her shoulders, the strands an untamed riotous mass. She walked with determination, her hips swaying seductively as she navigated the uneven flagstone patio. Her grace was even more remarkable given the unyielding leather dress and her crazy-high stilettos. Even though the shoes added extra height, she didn't look tall. In fact, he doubted she'd reach his chin.

A need to protect flared in him. The sensation was as unexpected as it was unwelcome.

On occasion, he played with women at Damien's home, known as the Den. Michael had been sexually attracted to many of them. But he'd only had this kind of visceral reaction one other time in his thirty years. He'd ignored his intuition and the warnings of others and had ended up married within three months.

A few years later, he and his bride had been in court, and he'd spent most of his inheritance to hold onto the Eagle's Bend Ranch. The two thousand acres had been in his family for over eighty years, and if he had lost it, he was certain his father would haunt him from the grave. The lessons Michael had learnt in rebuilding his life and fortune had made him harder, smarter and more wary.

He adjusted his cowboy hat and continued to look at the blonde. She had joined a group of people near the fire. Her figure-hugging dress did as much to arouse him as nudity would have.

Until this moment, he hadn't missed having a woman in his bedroom, tied to his rustic four-poster bed, arms and legs spread wide as she lay there for him, willing and waiting. Last night he'd gone to bed alone after masturbating to ease the day's tension. Tonight, he hoped things would be different. He was glad he hadn't simply tossed away the invitation to the Den's solstice party. Although, he admitted, if he took this woman home, he'd wish for a longer night rather than a longer day.

As if sensing his perusal, she glanced over her shoulder. They made eye contact for less than five seconds, but it was enough, more than enough for him.

He heard someone say, "She's trouble."

Michael blinked and reluctantly turned towards the newcomer, Gregorio, the Den's caretaker.

"Don't go there," Gregorio advised, coming to a stop in front of him.

But Michael was already thinking about her, despite the fact she didn't resemble the women who generally caught his eye. He preferred a more rounded, feminine form—a woman that could withstand the rigors of ranch life.

"Her name's Sydney Wallace," Gregorio said.

Michael was aware of Gregorio's voice, but his focus was elsewhere. Sydney. Unusual name. He let it roll around in his mind, imagined how it might sound when he said it aloud as he told her what to do.

"She used to dance nude in a cabaret in Vegas and has a boa constrictor as a pet. It killed her last Dom and dragged him out to the backyard. She's on the run from the law. We heard she's wanted in ten states and two Canadian provinces." Gregorio snapped his fingers near Michael's face, jarring him from his reverie. "You listening to me, Mike?"

"Huh?" He shook his head and looked at Gregorio.

"I figured you weren't listening, otherwise you'd have decked me for calling you Mike." Gregorio chuckled. "Seriously, if you want to play, there are a number of subs here tonight—they're wearing the house's purple wrist band. That means they're available for a scene, they know the rules and they follow them. Any one of them would be much better for you than Sydney."

Gregorio, as Damien Lowell's right-hand man, knew things. Gregorio understood human nature and, since he tracked all the membership applications, he had insider knowledge of everyone at the Den. He served as a house monitor and sometimes participated in scenes. Because he was so well respected, Doms and subs alike listened to him. Those who didn't often rued their decision.

For the first time, Michael wanted to ignore Gregorio's unsolicited advice. "I didn't see a collar around her neck." He took in the people she was standing with. "And she doesn't seem to be here with anyone."

"She doesn't have a Dom."

"I'll bite. What's wrong with Ms Wallace?"

"Other than the snake and the problems with the law?"

"What?" he asked, taking a drink of the light beer from his cup and looking back at her. A waiter approached with a tray full of sparkling water, and she snagged a flute. Her back was to him, and he couldn't drag his gaze away from her shapely derrière. "Is she a Domme?"

"She's a sub," Gregorio said, giving the answer Michael wanted. "But one with no real interest in a relationship with a man."

He blinked. "She's gay?" Please God, no, not now that he was imagining her legs wrapped around his waist as he drove into her wet pussy.

"She likes men just fine. What I mean is, she'll start playing, if a guy interests her. If he bores her, she bails."

"She'll leave in the middle of a scene?"

"It's happened a handful of times." Gregorio folded his arms across his chest. "She's earned the name the Brat around here."

"She sounds like a challenge," Michael said.

Gregorio laughed. The sound was both ominous and sympathetic. "A few other Doms have felt the same way," Gregorio said. "Sydney has a history of battering hearts and egos."

Water in hand, she walked around to the far side of the fire pit and stood there alone. He responded to the unspoken cue. After finishing his beer in a single gulp, he handed the empty glass to Gregorio. "Wish me luck."

Gregorio grinned. "You'll need more than luck, my friend."

Michael moved towards the fire pit.

Perhaps hearing his approach, she looked up and waited for him.

"Evening, ma'am," he said, as he stopped near her.

"I was hoping you would be brave enough to come and talk to me," she said with a smile that could roll his socks down. "I saw you talking with Gregorio. No doubt he tried to frighten you away with tales of how terrible I am."

"And are you?"

"I suppose there could be some truth to it." She shrugged easily. "But there's not. A good story is always better than the truth."

She smelt potently dangerous. The vanilla was mixed with unadulterated pheromones, and it was a cocktail he couldn't get enough of. "Either way, not much scares me."

"A man among men."

"Michael Dayton. Master Michael." Although the June sun hadn't completely vanished behind the distant mountain peaks, torches were being lit, adding to the ambience and catching streaks of red in her hair. He wanted to touch those strands, to curl them around his fist as he held her down and made her scream.

"Sydney Wallace," she said, returning the formality.

"May I call you Sydney?"

She rolled her glass between her palms. With a tease in her voice, she said, "I'm hoping you can be considerably more creative than that."

He tipped back the brim of his hat to get a better look at her. She intrigued him. "So name calling is not on your limits list."

A server, this one a woman in a French maid's outfit that left nothing to the imagination, walked nearby. Though she was curvy with luscious bare breasts, he only had eyes for the woman he was with.

Sydney placed her glass on the tray. He appreciated the fact she didn't need something to toy with.

When they were alone again, she said, "I understand you're divorced, Mr Dayton. No kids. You have a ranch you'd like to protect from gold diggers. You scene every once in a while, and you're not looking for a serious commitment."

"Do you know my blood type?"

She gave a quick grin. "No. I only asked about the important stuff."

"You found out a lot quickly."

"I like being prepared. If I'm going to spend an hour with a man, I want to make sure the time is worth it. I don't think it's fair to either of us if there are false expectations."

"You're mistaken, Sydney."

"About which part?"

"We'll be spending more than an hour together. I can't get you properly warmed up in under sixty minutes, and I intend to keep you on the edge, writhing for an orgasm for much, much longer than that."

Her eyes widened, and for the first time he noticed how blue they were, a shade of ice, a shocking contradiction to the heat she radiated.

"That's a brash statement, Michael."

He captured her chin gently. "Find out for yourself, Ms Wallace. Let's have an experiment here at the Den to see if we have chemistry. After that, we can head out to my ranch. It's about forty-five minutes from here. Or if you'd prefer, we can go to your place. Wherever you feel most comfortable." He noticed her legs were alluringly bare. He'd always been a stockings man. Or at least he had been. Until now. "Are you wearing underwear?"

"I..."

With his index finger, her stroked her cheekbone. "I asked you a question."

"Yes."

"What kind?"

She hesitated for a moment, and he wondered if she was going to answer or whether she was going to run. He held her lightly enough that her movements weren't restricted.

"Boy shorts," she said.

"Please remove them for me."

"Now? Here?"

"Maybe you're the one who should be afraid," he said quietly, "rather than me. Gregorio says you often bail out of scenes. I wondered at first if it was because Doms asked too much from you. But I'm thinking they probably don't ask enough. I've known you less than five minutes, but I've figured out you're assertive. You know what you want, but I'm guessing you're not always good at asking for it. Furthermore," he added, leaning closer towards her, "I'm willing to bet you're bored with anyone who isn't as aggressive as you are. Am I wrong about that?"

She shivered. Since the Colorado evening was mild and they were standing near the fire, he knew she couldn't be cold. So something he'd said had hit a nerve.

Surprising him, she unflinchingly met his gaze. "You're right about the fact I get bored easily," she admitted. She put her hand around his wrist. "And you're wrong if you think I'm afraid of anything."

"Fair enough. In that case, take off your panties." He released his grip on her chin and she let go of him. He stayed in place, physically and figuratively refusing to give her space.

He offered his arm and she held onto it while precariously balancing on her heels.

Finally, she straightened and looked at him as she dangled the pretty pink material from her index finger. Too late he realised he'd made a mistake by not asking to see them on her first. They material would probably stretch across her derrière, highlighting her butt cheeks perfectly.

He accepted the proffered underwear and stuffed the lace and nylon confection in his pocket. Who would have suspected that she wore something so pretty beneath black leather? "What are your limits?"

"I haven't found any," she said.

"Then you've been playing with the wrong Doms."

She shrugged. "That's possible. But maybe I'm tougher than you think."

"Perhaps," he agreed, but with some scepticism. His ex-wife had let him believe she wanted things raw, but the moment the ring had been placed on her finger, the figurative collar had come off her throat. "Humiliation?"

"I don't have a lot of experience with that."

"No one has made you stand in a corner with your nose pressed to the wall when you misbehaved?"

Her lips parted for a moment, just long enough for him to wonder how she tasted. He loved anticipation, enjoyed getting a woman so turned on she lost her inhibitions, but now, with Sydney, unaccustomed impatience nipped at him.

"I don't misbehave," she said with an impish grin.

He raised his eyebrows. "Never? Or have you not played with a Dom long enough to establish a relationship?"

She gave a soft sigh. "Would you like to psychoanalyse me, Michael? If so, can we sit down somewhere? But honestly, I'm not sure if I'll ever see you again, so I'd prefer we spend an enjoyable evening together."

"I don't rush. I just want to know you a bit better before we play together. I want to give you what you need, not just what you want."

"That's an interesting distinction."

"You might want wine, but need water," he said. "I want you completely satisfied."

"You're right. I kind of move from Dom to Dom," she said. "A man, any man, would complicate my lifestyle. Maybe you think that's selfish, but it's who I am. I was hoping that since you're a divorced man who doesn't want to go through another divorce, you'd be fine with a one-night stand."

"Ouch," he said. When she opened her lovely mouth to speak again, he held up a hand to silence her. To her credit, she shut up. "No, you don't have to watch your words. In fact, I prefer your honesty."

"Really?"

He nodded. "And I'm not against a relationship. I'm not, in theory, against marriage." Passing the land to his heirs would be nice. He had one sister, who had two girls. Despite the fact he had a couple of horses, none of his relatives had shown any interest in the ranch.

"Are you looking for something permanent now?"

"No," he said.

"Then if you'd like to play, I would, too." Seductively, sexily, she placed her palm over his crotch.

Heat seared through the denim. Except for lovers he'd been with a long time, no woman had been so bold. He wanted to cave to his baser instincts and take her here, now. Instead, he captured her hand and moved it away.

She pulled back, breaking his grip, and he knew she felt rejected. What man in his right mind would have stopped her? "Don't take it personally," he said. "Please. I will want you to do that in the future, and right now I want to be buried balls-deep in your hot cunt as you cry out my name."

Her eyes opened wide. She seemed more intrigued than shocked. "I want that, too," she admitted.

"We need to clear up a few things."

"Right. I have no STDs, I have no physical limitations. Oh, yes, and I have condoms in my purse. Large. And medium, just in case." She grinned. "I've been called an eternal optimist. I don't need that size as much as most men would have you believe."

He shook his head. The charming Ms Wallace was trying to goad him, and he appreciated her efforts. Rather than responding, he changed the subject, "Why do you scene?"

"Why?"

"You've thought about it, surely?"

"I guess I'm always wondering where my limits are, and I like to transcend them. I mountain climb. White water river raft. I did a triathlon, and I'm competing in a mud race in a couple of weeks, you know, running up a mountain then doing obstacle courses, under barbed wire, over a wooden wall. My team is doing it for charity."

He was forced to look at her more objectively. His initial urge had been to care for her. Now he wondered if she could kick his ass. Maybe Gregorio had been right to issue warnings. "What's your safe word?"

"Everest."

Of course it was.

"You don't need to know why."

"Okay." He figured he already knew, but he looked forward to her telling him tomorrow morning over coffee. "How about a code for slowing down?"

"I don't believe in that."

"In that case, we'll use the word caution."

She sighed. "If I have to have one, how about we use the word turtle?"

He thumbed his hat. "I think I've just been insulted."

"Not at all. That would be rude. I'm just saying that saying that turtles are slow."

Not only was she attractive, but quick-witted and intelligent. It had been a long time since a woman had appealed to him on multiple levels. "How do you feel about public play?"

She hesitated for a second. "I've never tried it."

"Are you willing to?"

"I suppose."

"I prefer a yes or no answer," he told her. "Unless you'd rather talk about it?"

"No. I mean yes."

"Yes, Sir."

"Yes, Sir," she dutifully repeated.

"Good girl."

He saw her grit her teeth, but she said nothing. He'd hit a nerve demanding she conform to the smallest of courtesies, and he'd remember that. "Do you like impact play?"

Before he could ask further questions, she said, "I find an open-handed spanking to be really pleasurable. I also like belts." She glanced at his waist.

Oh, yeah. He'd happily lay the leather across her rear.

She was quiet for a moment, maybe as discombobulated as he was. And he realised she had an air of vulnerability that she tried to hide. Others probably missed it, but he was glad he hadn't.

"I'm also fine with a shoe or a ruler," she said, her words a hurried rush as if she were attempting to cover the uncomfortable silence. "Anything, really. Feel free to be creative. I'm okay with a flogger, open to trying a bull whip and cane. There isn't a position I'm adverse to, over the knee, or a table, or a bed. Standing, kneeling over a spanking bench. Did I miss anything?"

"The Sir at the end of the sentence."

"Of course. Sir." She gave him another of her sunny smiles.

No wonder she ate other Doms for breakfast. She seemed so guileless, he'd bet it would be difficult for some men to hold her accountable. "Clamps?"

She nodded. "The harder the better. As you're probably gathering, I find it easier to get off when there's erotic pain involved."

"Anal plugs?"

She fidgeted then said, "If you insisted, I'd try it."

"No one has claimed your ass?" he asked, stunned.

"No."

That he would be the first to place something up there made him even harder, and his erection pressed against his jeans. He wanted to readjust his cock, but he reminded himself to focus on her. There were a few other things he needed to know before they got started. "Handcuffs?"

"Any kind of bondage," she said.

"I've haven't lassoed a woman." He paused. "Yet."

Her eyes widened. "Sounds interesting."

Michael was suddenly glad he'd ignored Gregorio's advice. The thought of dragging a helpless Sydney towards him thrilled him. If she were barefoot and naked, it would be all the better. "And actual sexual penetration?"

"Like I said, I have condoms. In assorted sizes. I have nothing communicable, I'm on the pill. Anything else you need to know?"

"That will cover it," he said wryly. "Likewise, I have a clean bill of health, but I also believe in covering all the bases. We'll use condoms."

When he said nothing else, she gave a little flip of her hair and turned away, heading towards the house.

"Where are you going, Sydney?"

She stopped and looked over her shoulder. With a puzzled frown, she said, "Inside." She moistened her lips quickly then added, "I thought that was what you wanted."

"Did I say so?"

"No." She returned to stand in front of him. "I apologise."

"I'm going to spank you over there." He nodded towards a short metal fence in the distance. It bordered the grassy area beyond the horseshoe pits, far enough that they'd have some privacy. Still, since it was lit by a number of solar lights and torches, anyone who wanted to watch could.

She glanced around, and he waited patiently.

At least a dozen people were outside, a small group gathered on one side of the fire pit. Some stood around high tables. Elsewhere, a woman sat on a porch swing while her male sub licked her boot.

Another evening at the Den. "I think you need reminding that I prefer to be addressed as Master Michael and Sir. When we play together, Sydney, I make the rules. I will be sure you understand them and agree with them, but once that happens, they will be enforced. Do you understand?"

"Yes, Sir," she whispered.

"Do you agree to address me the way I prefer?"

She nodded.

"Please pull your dress up to your waist."

She couldn't have taken more time. He didn't complain, though. Watching her was its own reward. She was softness and sensuality all wrapped within a woman who was temporarily his.

"Ah," he said when she was exposed. "Such a pretty little pussy. I like that it's shaved." He looked at her expectantly.

"Thank you, Sir."

Interesting, since he'd drawn harsher boundaries, she seemed softer, more compliant. Everything she said and did seemed to be a contradiction. "Please put your hands behind your neck and bring your chest forward."

She did. "Would you like me to take the dress off entirely, Sir?"

"I'd like you to do as you're told, Sydney. Nothing more. Are you able to comfortably spread your legs a little farther apart? You can take off your shoes if you need to."

When she was in position, more open, he slid a hand between her legs. Her response delighted him. "You're moist, Sydney."

He kept his hand still, but she moved her hips a bit, sliding herself against him. "I generally won't mind if you come without permission. In fact, the more you orgasm, the more I get into the scene," he said. "But not tonight. Tonight I want you more aroused than you've ever been." He waited until she let out a tiny moan then he pulled his hand away. Before she could react, he slapped her cunt, hard.

She screamed and pitched forward slightly. He caught her and held her against him longer than necessary, liking the way they fit together.

For a moment, she stayed there before drawing in a deep breath and moving away. "*That* was unexpected. And unbelievably hot, Sir."

"Turtle?"

"No. More like that, please."

"Stay where you are. I'll be right back."

He went inside. Brandy, a sub who regularly helped with house functions and parties, fetched him a blanket and two separate cuffs.

"My pleasure, Sir," she said when he thanked her.

When he went back outside, Sydney was still in the same place. She was shifting from side to side a bit nervously, but she'd yet to bail out of the scene. "Are you doing okay?"

"Feeling a little exposed," she admitted. "Sir."

"Seeing you when I came back outside pleased me."

She visibly exhaled.

"Would you like to continue on?"

"Yes, Sir. I'm not scared," she said, but her voice didn't sound as sure it had earlier.

He nodded. "In that case, when you're ready, walk over to the fence." Then he scowled. "Are you okay in those shoes?"

"Completely."

"Good. I'll stay a step or two behind you so I can watch your ass move."

The view was all he'd hoped for. There was grace and sultry elegance in her every step. But when she reached the edge of the paved patio, he took her elbow. He helped her over the uneven terrain then draped the blanket over the rail.

Without being told, she kicked off the shoes and positioned herself, even remembering to spread her legs wide. No doubt this was a woman who knew what she wanted. And, whether or not she recognised it, by having her beautifully curved ass upturned and waiting for his attention she was already giving him what he wanted.

"Use your safe word if it's too much, your slow word if you're uncomfortable or get a muscle cramp. We can get you readjusted."

"Yes, I understand."

"Your choice, I can secure your legs in place or I can cuff your wrists."

She answered unhesitatingly. "I'd prefer you fasten my ankles so I can't get away, Sir."

"I'll expect you to keep your hands wrapped around the bars."

"Yes, of course, Sir."

He crouched to attach the cuffs, and he inhaled the heady scent of her muskiness. Keeping her turned on without letting her come was going to be exquisite. To test the bonds, he trailed his fingers up the insides of her thighs. She squirmed and pulled and yet she helplessly remained where he wanted her. Sometime in the future, he'd stick a plug up her ass too, to intensity her sensations. "I'm going to warm you up with a few spanks," he informed her. "Then I'll make you beg for more."

"You sound sure of yourself, Sir," she said, her voice muffled.

"I am, Sydney."

"You know, Sir, I have never begged for anything my entire life."

"And you've never been spanked by me."

About the Author

Sierra Cartwright was born in Manchester, England and raised in Colorado. Moving to the United States was nothing like her young imagination had concocted. She expected to see cowboys everywhere, and a covered wagon or two would have been really nice!

Now she writes novels as untamed as the Rockies, while spending a fair amount of time in Texas…where, it turns out, the Texas Rangers law officers don't ride horses to roundup the bad guys, or have six-shooters strapped to their sexy thighs as she expected. And she's yet to see a poster that says Wanted: Dead or Alive. (Can you tell she has a vivid imagination?)

Sierra wrote her first book at age nine, a fanfic episode of Star Trek when she was fifteen, and she completed her first romance novel at nineteen. She actually kissed William Shatner (Captain Kirk) on the cheek once, and she says that's her biggest claim to fame. Her adventure through the turmoil of trust has taught her that love is the greatest gift. Like her image of the Old West, her writing is untamed, and nothing is off-limits.

She invites you to take a walk on the wild side…but only if you dare.

Sierra Cartwright loves to hear from readers. You can find her contact information, website details and author profile page at http://www.total-e-bound.com.

Total-E-Bound Publishing

www.total-e-bound.com

Take a look at our exciting range of literagasmic™
erotic romance titles and discover pure quality
at Total-E-Bound.

CPSIA information can be obtained at www.ICGtesting.com
Printed in the USA
BVOW03s0723020116

431602BV00001B/18/P